Echo of Lies

Alice Baburek

PublishAmerica
Baltimore

ISBN: 1-60836-592-1
PUBLISHED BY PUBLISHAMERICA, LLLP
www.publishamerica.com
Baltimore

Printed in the United States of America

This book is dedicated to the staff at Suburban Animal Hospital located in Parma, Ohio. Their continuous devotion and perpetual commitment for the care and well being of animals surpasses and soars far beyond the calls of a veterinarian practice. A heart-filled thanks to Dr. Mary Schroth, Dr. William Clark, Judy, Tracy, Pat and Chrissie, who have shown repeatedly their true allegiance to the wellness of animals.

I also would like to acknowledge my loving partner, Cindy, who endlessly supports my writing endeavors. And to my special and dear friends, Maria Shinn, LLC, and Sherry Fry whose friendship I cherish and hold close to my heart.

Suzanne,

Thank you again for
your support. I hope you
enjoy the book! Keep
reading!

Anne
"2009"

PROLOGUE

Voices echoed aimlessly inside my head. My heart was racing while my palms had become coated with sweat. I frantically searched inside myself to find the hidden truth that would set me free. Free from my doubts and inhibitions. Free from what my life had become and now rested in the hands of twelve faceless and nameless people. Twelve people who hadn't a clue about the person I had become. Twelve people who would never understand the atrocity of how human error could erode and dissolve a person's life in an instant. Twelve people who held the power to change my life, forever. Twelve people...

CHAPTER 1

It seemed like a lifetime ago when we first met. I was assigned to assist in one of the most important murder investigations since the turn of the century. Whether it was by default or because I was the highest-ranking woman in the division, really didn't matter much to me. What did matter was that I would be directly involved in one of the most bizarre cases ever recorded in the history of the FBI.

It read nothing like a typical textbook serial killer case. This time it was much different. It wasn't the fact that each of these women died a gruesome and violent death. No, sadly enough, it was the fact, that while alive, every single one of them had shared something in common—considerable net worth by either prominent positions or association.

It had been a long painstaking year since the first body was discovered. Since then, averaging about one a month, a new victim would surface and be added to the unending total. Evidence had been collected and analyzed. Leads had been followed to the point of exhaustion. Still, the killer remained at large; doing what he did best, killing.

But it wasn't until the latest fatality had been positively identified and her name plastered across the tabloids of America that pushed to solve this case way beyond its priority status. This unfortunate victim was not really a rich woman in terms of money, but rich in the sense of association.

Linda Haley, had been the President's niece; a young attractive lesbian who had been idolized and respected by gay communities across the nation. With the flamboyant openness of her prominent gay lifestyle, along with her heroic efforts for the perseverance of equal rights, she had opened the door to discriminative publicity and many times unwarranted threats. Haley's widely acclaimed determination to make this a better country, enticed her to be the forth runner for the introduction and promotion of legislation for same sex marriages. Sadly enough and ill-starred, came the misconstrued and distorted image of homosexuality which not only played into her eventual downfall, but hinted to her untimely death.

Rumors spread quickly and fingers pointed to the unethical involvement of the Presidential Office. Media broadcasted an ugly truth on how the U.S. President (her uncle) was far from being an advocate of gay rights. And who could ever forget the Senator's infamous speech during his well publicized Presidential elect campaign.

"If I am elected President, I promise you this: it will be a cold day in hell before this country will ever conceivable recognize, let alone accept and acknowledge, same sex marriages!"

Resentful rallies entailed and protest marches were frequented becoming a permanent part of the illustrious scenery on Capitol Hill. It was quite obvious then this particular President Wannabe would not win the hearts or the votes of the gay population. But, as fate would have it, none of that would matter. The Senator had won the Presidential seat, even with the uprising of thousands of homosexual voices, by what the political system coined the term "a landslide." The demands of the majority and straight had spoken as it left behind the voiceless votes that represented an insignificant piece of the American pie.

And so that is why Lena Harris came with bursting authority as a noted prestige representative directly from the White House staff. Appointed by the newly elected President himself, Harris immediately seized command of the botched investigation and made it decisively clear who indeed was in charge. Harris' superior demeanor and persistent determination was a whirling run-off from her former military years as one of the highest-ranking women officers in the corp. Harris was more than just tough according to the male definition of the word. Her large framed body moved with ease as her aura of over confidence purposely cleared a path ahead. And when Harris bellowed her boisterous and demanding voice, she would instantly captivate her audience and immediately become the center of attention.

As with anything else, Lena Harris wasn't afraid of challenges. In fact, she welcomed them. Lena wasted little time setting up the ground rules and perimeters for the special elite task force. Fifteen top field agents and ten support personnel were meticulously selected to work on this over glorified manhunt. I, of course, had been chosen as one of them.

It wasn't until after our first long and tedious meeting, Lena gave way and acknowledged my actual existence. I could sense Lena's hesitance as she approached me. Maybe she felt a bit intimidated, because I too, had been a woman accredited with many accomplishments and notable achievements during my tenure with the FBI. But I highly doubted the word even existed in Harris' ego centric vocabulary. All in all, my background and credentials were no secret and neither was my sexuality.

"Agent Becker, join me for lunch," commanded Lena Harris. The stuffy conference room had emptied leaving me very little choice for refusal.

"As you insist," I replied reluctantly.

It wasn't long before we arrived at the diner which had already been consumed by lunching regulars. The wait for a single table could turn into more than just a few minutes. I could tell by her constant shifting, patience was not one of Lena's stronger virtues.

"We could eat somewhere else." I was hoping she would jump at my suggestion or call off this whole ordeal. Just then the hostess announced the availability of seats.

The dismal wintry sky shed little light through the tinted windows. It was a dreary, long day so far and I didn't see any change for the remainder of the afternoon. Lena remained silent as she quickly scanned the restaurant's menu. My eyes seemed drawn to Lena's unusual attractiveness she shed so easily without the slightest intention. Within moments, a server arrived at the table.

"I'm ready," she boasted never missing a beat while she quickly proceeded to order her lunch. Caught off guard by her abruptness and odd behavior, I hurriedly searched the menu for something easy and digestible.

"What do you do for fun when you're not pretending to be an FBI agent?" Instantly, my thoughts went blank as my superior tried to peek into and retrieve some information about my personal life. For a brief moment, I was a little on edge at the notion of where this conversation might be leading.

"Do you like to dance?" she asked not waiting for any particular response. Lena's dark mysterious eyes made me feel a bit unsettled. I tried to swallow, but an enormous lump formed deep within my throat.

"Yes, as a matter of fact I do." Then suddenly, Lena's stare became hollow. There was something not quite right about her and I just couldn't put my finger on it. I was a true believer when it came to first impressions and the impact left behind. Once again, our conversation lapped into silence. Both lunches were served within a reasonable amount of time considering the large crowd of people gathered inside the diner.

"Alix, I want you to work directly with me. We need to move quickly and solve these murders. So, I am going to bypass the task force on certain aspects of this investigation. If you're as smart as I think you are, you'll do as I say without asking a bunch of nonessential questions." Lena graciously wiped her mouth with the white paper napkin. I was slightly confused by Lena's strict restrictions, yet felt a bit honored she had requested my expertise. Or did she? Oddly enough, I found myself intrigued, yet hesitant in getting to know this bewildering woman.

"If that's the way you want to conduct this investigation, I have no…" My sentence was rudely cut-off in midstream.

"Alix, let me make things simple and perfectly clear. In the President's eyes, *I AM* the task force. Me and only me! The rest of those insignificant bodies are to pacify a few over zealous government officials who believe that the FBI should be given a second chance. That's it—nothing more, nothing less." Her voice was deep and threatening.

"So, what will it be? It wouldn't hurt to boost your sagging career by sticking close to my side. Who knows, if you play your cards right, you might just end up in Washington D.C.!" Lena's light brown tousled hair danced about with any slight movement of her head. It was then the server returned with the check and placed it near Lena's plate. She stared at it for a brief moment then slid it to me.

"Do we understand one another, Alix?" Lena's persona had many different and annoying faces.

"And for an added incentive…" Under the round wooden table, Lena's warm leg brushed lightly against mine. Instinctively, I shifted in my seat and remained quiet.

"Why do I sense a bit of apprehension from you about my proposal, Alix?" Surprisingly, Lena slid her chair closer to mine. Her dark eyes seemed to lighten and actually glistened in the fading skylight. Then unexpectedly, Lena firmly grasped my leg with her strong hand. My mind and body collided as I desperately tried to sort through the rush of overwhelming feelings. Bewildered and amazed by this display of flamboyant behavior, I knew beyond a shadow of a doubt, this was a definite play on my sexuality.

"Good, by your silence I will assume we have a mutual understanding!" Lena stood up to take leave. I remained seated for a moment and waited for the blood to sink from my reddened face.

With nothing left to say, Lena turned on her heel and made her way out the door. As I headed to the Bureau car alone, I tried to organize my clouded thoughts. It wasn't long after I arrived back at work when I received a startling email from Lena.

> **Dear Alix,**
>
> **I enjoyed your company at lunch today. Between the two of us I know we're going to make a difference. I'm looking forward to it!**
>
> **LH**

The message was short, sweet and to the point. Could this actually be happening to me? I had no choice, but to go along with Lena's personal and work related expectations, even if it meant stripping away a small piece of my dignity to maintain her over inflated alter ego.

CHAPTER 2

The weekend crept in with unseasonably warm weather. I finished my rounds of errands and tried to spend some quality time reading an abandoned novel. But my thoughts kept flashing back to Lena and her unwanted advances. As the evening hours rolled in, I felt a bit of nervous energy I just couldn't shake. So after redressing in black jeans and a purple silk blouse, I headed out for a bit of welcomed company at the Peastone.

Sandy Lewis, a relatively close friend of mine, had been tending bar when I entered the smoke filled room. Immediately, her vivid blue eyes sparkled and danced with delight at the sight me.

"What brings you out on a night like this?" she questioned with a huge grin. Sandy was not much taller than me, but definitely construed with more feminine attributes for an out-and-about lesbian.

"You're not happy to see me?" I acknowledged by displaying a sad face. Sandy's smile radiated happiness piercing straight through the dim light. The softness of her bleached blond hair fell gently against the sides of her slim and attractive face.

"You know better, Alix, it's always a pleasure when you come in to visit and sit at my bar," replied Sandy with a quick squeeze to my hand. I had been attracted to Sandy from the first moment I met her almost two years ago. Her genuine personality and warm heart struck a deep chord inside. My face blushed so easily.

"You still thinking about us?" she shyly asked. I wishfully tried to will away my embarrassment.

"No…I just thought…" My words tumbled over my tongue. Without hesitation, I hurriedly sipped at my mixed drink Sandy had so graciously placed in front of me.

Sandy batted her long eyelashes then continued to wait on customers at the far end of the bar. I thought for a moment and contemplated her vague insinuation of branding us to be more than just friends.

"Well, hello, Alix," broadcasted a strong and familiar voice. Suddenly, I could feel the warmth of her breath against the back of my neck. Lena Harris had pulled up a bar stool and sat only inches away.

"So…you do get out and play? And I see you've already met my close and extremely devoted friend, Sandy Lewis." Sandy threw Lena a pitiful glance. I couldn't believe that Lena and Sandy knew one another. Not once, in all of our chit-chatting over the past couple of years, did Sandy ever mention the name of Lena Harris. But then again, did she have to?

"Why Alix, you look shocked as if the cat got your pretty little tongue!" Lena pushed even harder.

"I guess you might be even more surprised by the fact Sandy and I use to be a happy couple long ago!" Her wicked smirk was frightening. I eagerly turned away just to hear some type of denial from Sandy. But by the sorrowful look on Sandy's face, I knew it to be the unforgiving truth.

"I'm not as bad you think, Alix. In fact, I can be quite pleasurable at times…isn't that right, Sandy?" Lena's hand began massaging the inside of my muscular leg. For a brief moment, I felt hurt and betrayed.

"I won't bite unless you want me too," she cackled while motioning to Sandy for a drink.

"Lena, that's enough! Why don't you try a little harder to control your sudden urges?" questioned an angry Sandy. By the sudden turn of facial expressions, it was obvious Lena did not appreciate Sandy's stern tone.

"Sandy, you above all, know not to dissuade me!" Lena withdrew her groping fingers from my nervous leg. Sandy leaned in close at the same time the music grew louder.

"You don't own me, Lena!" Sandy tossed the damp rag into Lena's lap. Lena angrily threw back the dirty towel onto the bar.

"You'll be sorry!" threatened Lena as she stood up and disappeared out the door. Sandy's eyes suddenly filled with tears.

"I just sealed my own coffin," she sobbed.

"I'm sorry, Alix, I should have told you that I knew Lena and now, it's too late." Despair covered her lovely face.

"It's alright, Sandy. I wouldn't worry about Lena's empty threats." I tried to comfort this gentle and caring woman.

"They're not empty, Alix. You don't *know* the real Lena Harris!" Sandy frantically wiped away her tears then retreated further behind the bar.

"Sandy! Wait! We need to talk!" I shouted desperately over the increasing beat of the music. Sandy shook her head back-and-forth then pulled away.

I felt unsettled leaving things as they were with Sandy. I took the initiative and decided to try and reach her one last time. I wrote my personal cell phone number down on a piece of paper and asked a young woman to delivery the message to the barmaid. I watched from a distance and saw that Sandy shoved the note inside her pocket. At least Sandy did not throw the note away. I took this to be a good sign.

I wasn't home more than a few minutes before the call came in; amazingly enough, it was Sandy.

"Alix, I'm sorry for the way I acted tonight. But you just can't imagine…the magnitude of atrocities…and Lena…!" Her voice trailed into a whisper.

"Explain to me so I will understand," I insisted.

"Meet me at the coffee house on 7th and Huron tomorrow at six o'clock." And before I could respond to her invitation, the call had abruptly ended.

The secretive dilemma surrounding Lena Harris tweaked more than just my curiosity. I desperately needed to unravel the mystery which enveloped this powerful woman. And Sandy Lewis just might be the person to help me.

CHAPTER 3

The quaint and charming coffee house greeted its customers with a genuine invitation to relax and enjoy its home-like cozy surroundings. The blazing fireplace accoutered an intimate area for those who were avid readers and took delight in such a tranquil atmosphere.

Immediately, I visually connected with Sandy. There in a wooden booth stationed far back in the corner of the room, Sandy sat alone. The twinkle which once danced freely within her carefree eyes had suddenly vanished leaving behind a pool of emptiness. She cleared her voice then spoke in a low tone.

"You have to realize, Alix, what I am about to tell you goes way beyond the world of secrecy. If certain people ever found out I told you this information, both you and I would be in grave danger. I don't want to even think about the horrible, horrible consequences we could both suffer if we were careless." Sandy's fear was intense and real. My hand instinctively covered hers. She closed her eyes and I silently waited for her to begin. Sandy sighed heavily before she decided to delve into my confidence.

"Alix, you couldn't even imagine how many influential people there are in this massive political arena who are involved one way or another. These people can use their power to hurt us, Alix. No one is indispensable." Sandy stopped and took a quick drink from her sweating water glass.

"Sandy, you lost me already," I stated a bit confused.

"I'm sorry, Alix, I'm getting ahead of myself. Let me start at the beginning," replied Sandy.

"I had just enlisted in the military when I first met her. She was a drill instructor at boot camp." Sandy hesitated, again, as if she was collecting her thoughts before she continued on.

"So your commanding officer happened to be Lena Harris?" I asked not meaning to interrupt so soon.

"Yes. Lena had been assigned to the women's recruit camp. Tough as nails but she loved the ladies. New recruits were considered 'fresh' and were unsuspecting subjects for her roaming eyes and eager hands. Most of the cadets were young and naïve and didn't know how to handle her sexual advances. They dare not speak against the commanding officer. I knew enough to know that this certain drill instructor was going way beyond the call of duty. Lena would periodically try to conceal her unmistakable attraction to females by associating with top ranking male officers. What a cover, so she thought. I could see right through her feminist façade since the very first day. Everyone knows that the military frowns upon gays. Nothing was ever resolved with Clinton's 'don't ask, don't tell' policy. Tension still exists for gays who remain silent and it can be downright dangerous for those who are brave enough to speak out about their sexual preference." Sandy barely sipped at her ice water. She played with the straw as she contemplated her words.

"With the assistance of a few influential male and female high-ranking officers, Lena forged ahead with her own private agenda. It was during my very last week in boot camp, rumors of Lena becoming a commissioned officer swept the barracks like wildfire." Sandy suddenly cleared her throat and glanced about the coffee house. I eagerly waited with anticipation for her to continue with her story.

"Lena took a liking to me from the first day. I was smart enough to know she was hitting on me. Don't get me wrong, Alix, I had to admit I found her to be quite exciting and different in a rough and raw kind of a way. For a cadet to have a highly decorated officer show such an intense interest is more than just flattering. But I did debate whether to act on these sexual whims or try to keep her at bay. On one hand, I knew if I didn't cooperate, Lena could make my stay in the military a living nightmare. Believe me, Alix, it was an arduous decision I had to face. I gave in and became Lena's playmate. Well, instead of reaping the benefits that come with sleeping with the boss, it turned out to be quite the opposite. She even went as far as humiliating me during a surprise barracks inspection." Sandy gave a slight chuckle.

"I came awful close to a dishonorable discharge. I couldn't let this happen to me. I worked too hard and too long to let this conniving, evil woman destroy me." Sandy stopped speaking for a brief moment.

"Anyhow, by the time I received my orders, she had me reassigned to work with her on a special project." Sandy closed her eyes.

"I couldn't break free from her choking grip! It didn't take long before her demands became too much for me and then…came the abuse. I was so afraid of what she could do to me, Alix. After two long years under her vise like control, I couldn't take it any more. I had no dignity, no self respect…so I did the only thing I could…I left the military." Sandy dropped her head upon her chest. My heart went out to Sandy. I just couldn't imagine living each day with such extreme trauma. Just then the server approached our booth.

"You sure I couldn't get either of you ladies something to eat?" Her youthful appearance gave the coffee house a bit of fresh air. Both of us cordially declined and the disappointed server once again, left us alone.

"Needlesstosay, Lena was not very receptive when she found out about my willingness to end my military career to a whim." Sandy's knuckles turned white as she wrapped her hand around the half-filled glass.

"I thought leaving the service would put an end to the tightening noose she held around my neck. But I was so wrong. Lena eventually moved on and became a prominent symbol and a shining example for all women, not just for those serving in the armed forces. She went even as far as getting a spot on the cover of *Newsweek* and *Cosmopolitan* representing the typical American woman! Lena's love for attention kept inflating that overwhelming ego of hers and unfortunately, tightening the hold she had on me. I kept relocating from one place to another, just hoping and praying that she would eventually forget about me, but Lena made sure she found me each and every time." Sandy put her hand to her cheek and wiped away the droplets of tears.

"It wasn't long before she cashed in on her glamorous publicity. First as a CIA agent and then she decided to climb even higher to become one of the top aides to the President. With this new prestigious position, I was so sure, now, she'd have to let me go!" Sandy's hand lightly began to tremble.

"My life had become a living nightmare. I couldn't sleep, I couldn't eat, I couldn't even hold down a steady job! And as for any type of romantic relationship…well, it was no use. Lena made sure she kept me close at hand." Sandy hung her head in sorrow.

"I'm sorry, Sandy," is all I could say to this wondrous woman.

"My physical appearance began to deteriorate. I began to drink heavily to try and drowned out my pitiful life. I hid indoors. She…she had eyes, everywhere!"

Sandy shifted nervously. For a brief moment, she closed her eyes as if she was shutting out the horrible images of becoming a tormented prisoner.

"Have you ever lived in constant fear, Alix? Have you ever been afraid to close your eyes at night because you may not wake up in the morning? Wondering what new living hell awaited you as you climbed out of bed each insignificant day?" Sandy's hand turned into a fist.

"I made a huge mistake and have been paying for it with my life." The look of despair completely consumed Sandy's face as her bottom lip began to quiver. Sandy appeared to be exhausted as if all her energy had been sucked from within her body.

"Alix, do you remember about three or four years ago when a woman agent was killed in the line of duty? She was working with the CIA on a highly sensitive case; it was an overseas drug operative mission." Immediately, my throat went dry. I knew the agent very well. In fact, at one time, she was my partner.

"Alix, I know about the affair you had with that agent." With great surprise by her choice of words, I shifted uneasily in my seat.

"It wasn't an affair," were all the words I could muster. The shock from this conversation suddenly overwhelmed me.

"Those were Lena's words, not mine. I know you don't want to hear this, Alix, but it was Lena who helped…your friend break the case wide open. In fact, Lena made sure your friend's cover remained secure. Lena had power when she was involved with the CIA." Sandy seemed to pull herself together a bit. I, on the other hand, was quickly unraveling at the seams. For some strange reason, I began to feel sick. Why didn't I know about this before? Rita and I shared everything, or so I thought. How naïve and stupid…and now I could add feeling like a complete fool to the bottom of the list.

"So what you are telling me is that Rita and Lena worked with one another?" My voice turned rigid with disbelief.

"Yes," whispered Sandy.

"Alix, are you okay?" Sandy's voice was comforting. I knew she was telling the truth. How many more secrets had been kept from me? Unfortunately, I was about to find out.

"I think there's something else you should know about your…friend. Her name wasn't Rita Simfirt. It was Susanne Lanquist. She remained undercover even when she was with you. If you knew her true identity, well, it could have jeopardized the whole operation. I'm so sorry, Alix." Instantly, my heart felt heavy. Sandy gently patted my hand.

"Some people can put on a great façade, Alix. But that doesn't mean the feelings Suzanne felt for you weren't genuine and true." Sandy remained quiet.

"What does it matter now? She's dead." I felt my emotions slipping away. I never bothered to give myself the chance to grief and heal the way I should have for my departed friend and partner.

Sandy looked away for an instant. I knew there had to be something more Sandy wasn't telling me. She was holding back and I desperately needed to hear the entire truth.

"What else do you know and are not telling me?" I questioned. Sandy's eyes were sad. She bit her lower lip then casually looked down at the table.

"I don't know exactly how to say this, but Suzanne is not…dead. She's still alive, Alix." Within that fraction of a second, it was as if Sandy had just slapped me violently across the face.

"It's impossible. She died in an explosion!" By now mixed emotions crept in and took control as my eyes brimmed with tears ready to spill.

"Yes, there was an explosion and a body was found. But it wasn't Suzanne. I don't know whose body it was. It was staged so Suzanne could enter the witness protection program. They were afraid that even after the mission she would still be targeted for execution." Sandy leaned back in the booth.

"How could you possibly know all of this information?" I asked fighting back the tears. Sandy shrugged her shoulders.

"Lena," is all she said. I urgently tried to make sense of what I had just been told.

"You still don't get it, do you? Lena is like an out-of-control locomotive that can't be stopped! She will destroy anyone who crosses her path!" Sandy's breathing quickened.

"Why are you telling me all of this?" I closed my eyes with regret.

"Don't you see? Now, she has her sights set on you! You can see it when she looked at you, Alix, at the bar last night." Sandy appeared forlorn and concerned.

"Is that it? Or is there more I should know?" I wanted to finish up with Sandy and leave. I needed to be alone. Sandy began to fidget. She slowly looked about the coffee shop.

"She knows about the murders," whispered Sandy. Now I was really confused, but intrigued.

"Of course, she does. Lena was assigned by the President to head the task force. That's a given." I was puzzled by such an odd comment.

"I mean *she knows* about the murders!" Sandy leaned in close for me to hear.

"This woman is pure evil, Alix. Don't ever, ever underestimate the extent of her power." Sandy's eyes darted back and forth.

"Are you saying what I think you're saying?" I was dumbstruck by such a notion.

"Yes," answered Sandy. We both knew the significance of these allegations without saying the words out loud.

"You need to be careful, Alix. Do not trust anyone!" Sandy glanced at her watch.

"I've got to go." And before I could add to the conversation, Sandy slipped out of the booth and disappeared through the back door. I sat alone for a brief moment trying to digest the information Sandy had just divulged. If what she had told me was the absolute truth, I was in for one of the biggest challenges I would ever come to face in my entire life.

CHAPTER 4

I arrived at work early Monday morning. Lena's car was parked in the VIP designated spot. It didn't take long before the entire Task Force was together, once again, crammed into one of the larger secure meeting rooms. Lena looked sharp dressed in her tailored black slacks and gray pin striped blouse. Her small tight curls hung loosely along the sides of her well defined slender face. Her body movements were deliberate. When she wanted attention, she got it. I watched her carefully for quite some time. I despised the fact she had worked with Rita or should I say Suzanne.

"In conclusion, please direct your questions and/or concerns to Agent Becker." With the mention of my name, I was immediately snapped back to the present.

"I want a full detailed report from each of the subcommittees by the end of the week." Lena gathered her folders in a neat pile. I turned and merged into the receding group as members of the group slowly staggered into the hallway.

"Agent Becker, I would like to have a few words with you." Several people glanced my way as I waited patiently by the side of the main table. Within minutes, the room had finally emptied leaving the two of us alone.

"You wanted to speak to me?" I ask innocently. Lena slowly closed the door and locked it from the inside. She turned abruptly and faced me.

"You didn't hear a word I said, did you?" accused Lena. I paused before answering.

"Actually, no," I replied honestly. Lena's eyes narrowed with anger.

"I thought, Agent Becker, we had a mutual understanding?" She lightly ran her fingertip along the contour of my rigid face. My instinct was to pull back, but I knew I could not without a fight. I desperately wanted Lena to realize that I was not afraid of her erroneous claim to fame.

"You judge me too harshly, Agent Becker. I can see by your eyes that you don't trust me. Are you afraid of me?" Lena's words oozed with superiority. I firmly stood my ground and did not back down.

"No, I'm not afraid of you, Lena, should I be?" I threw the question right back into her lap and this seemed to wipe the smirk completely from her devilish face. Breaking eye contact, Lena quickly turned her back to me.

"It's Special Agent Harris to you, Becker," boasted Lena with authority.

"And before you can protest, I was indeed given the rank of special agent, out of courtesy, from the FBI Director, Curtiss Waitfield." Lena chuckled softly.

"By the way, did you enjoy your playful little visit with Sandy yesterday?" Lena's cynicism was well detected. I wasn't completely surprised by her knowledge of the meeting.

"Will that be all, Special Agent Harris?" I decided not to feed into her over zealous confidence. Lena turned to face me with tightly drawn lips then hissed a verbal warning.

"You have no idea, no idea, Agent Becker, who you are dealing with and if I were you, I would watch my back. Some people are not who they seem to be!" And with that said she roughly pushed me aside, unlocked the door and left.

It seemed as if Lena had purposely avoided contact with me during the remainder of the week after our "little talk" in the conference room. Sandy called to confirm my suspicions that the both of us were being watched. Next time, Sandy and I would have to be more careful and much more discreet when we decided to meet again.

As it would seem, efforts from the task force proved to be futile. Even with Lena's boisterous exclamation of finding the killer, it gave no ground to any new leads or uncovered any new evidence that might bring the investigation, even a tad closer to catching this horrendous murderer.

I was told that the President was notably unhappy and dissatisfied with Lena's official reports. In response to her inability to solve this unruly case in a timely manner, the President felt he had been left with no other choice, but to appoint yet another top field agent to this blundering investigation. Lena became absolutely furious when the news came down straight from oval office at the White House.

Within minutes of the field agent's arrival, a special briefing was called to order. Lena's adversary was dressed to kill. Her tight fitted black silk suit complimented her shapely hips and muscular legs. Blond highlights flowed freely throughout her short to long dark brown hair. But it was her Native American smooth complexion and her vitalizing blue-green eyes, which captivated my complete attention.

She cleared her throat then meticulously adjusted the mike to fit her six foot frame which filled the entire space behind the podium. I couldn't help but to stare in admiration while at the same time ingest the energy released from within her radiating aura. Butterflies danced freely inside as I eagerly focused on this intriguing and beautiful woman. Then by surprise, she quickly glanced about the room and unexpectedly made brief eye contact with me. I felt the rush of heat rise instantly to my awestruck face.

"Good afternoon; my name is Special Agent Sierra Montgomery. I have been assigned to assist all of you, in a joint effort, with solving the multi-murder investigation. It has been noted by a higher authority that this Task Force has reached a standstill." She briefly looked down at her papers. No one moved nor made a sound. She flipped several pages back and forth. She continued on with poise and essence of authority.

"Special Agent Lena Harris and I will be reviewing all the information on each of the murders. Reassignment of subcommittees will be forthcoming. Thank you for your attention and cooperation." Special Agent Sierra Montgomery immediately closed the file and turned abruptly to leave. I sat awestruck and amazed by the penetrating directness of this brusque wonderful woman. Various descriptive words popped into my head, but the word "WOW" captured it all. As the room slowly emptied of its audience, Special Agent Montgomery slipped silently back inside the room unnoticed.

"Agent Becker, I presume." Special Agent Montgomery held out her long slim fingers. My eyes quickly went from her "drop dead gorgeous" eyes to her outstretched slender hand. For an awkward moment, I stood without moving or making a sound. She patiently waited for me to reciprocate.

"Yes, yes, I am Agent Alixandria Becker. It is a pleasure to meet you, Special Agent Montgomery." I tried desperately not to stumble over my words, but my nerves began to jump from the electrifying touch emanating from this amazing woman.

"I was informed of your in-depth knowledge regarding the details of this investigation. I would like for us to discuss the specifics of where the Task Force actually stands in relation to catching this killer," she requested. Her thin lips were enticing. But before Special Agent Montgomery gave me a chance to respond, she continued on with yet another request.

"How about three o'clock this afternoon? We can meet in one of the small conference rooms," she casually asked.

"Sure, no problem." I stood for a moment and immediately Special Agent Montgomery took notice of my hesitation.

"Is there anything else, Agent Becker?" she questioned with a half grin.

"Well, yes, there is if I may be frank with you, Special Agent Montgomery?" I shifted nervously from one foot to the other. Special Agent Montgomery slightly raised her left brow at my abruptness.

"Okay, let's get rid of the formality. Please call me Sierra as I will call you, Alix. Agreed?" I nodded in silence.

"If you don't mind me asking, why do you want to meet with me when Special Agent Harris is the head of the Task Force and is highly acclimated with the investigation?" I questioned with puzzlement. Special Agent Montgomery did not answer, but licked her lower lip then grinned.

"See you at three, Alix." With that direct order she quietly left the room.

The next couple of hours flew by and I hurriedly prepared my report for the upcoming meeting with Sierra. When I entered the semi-dark room, a faint hint of perfume lingered in the cool conference room air. It was a pleasant scent that heightened my senses. For some strange reason, I felt a bit uneasy. It was then I noticed a thin line of light seeping from underneath the bathroom door. Within a moment of my realization, Sierra casually strolled out unaware of my presence. I silently watched from within the shadows overwhelmed by her gracefulness. She purposefully stopped then carefully ran her hands slowly up and down her shapely muscular legs flattening out the slight creases. Unexpectedly, my heart began to beat a bit faster as I gazed upon her loveliness. Suddenly, without any warnings, she flipped on the switch. The fluorescent lights blazed down illuminating the entire sitting area. I felt embarrassed by my childish behavior.

"Do you always stand in the dark unannounced?" Sierra stood tall with her hands placed firmly on her curved hips. For a brief moment, I did not know how to respond.

"No, not unless it's necessary," I replied while trying desperately to think of something else to say.

"I'm sorry, I didn't mean to startle you," I said apologetically. Sierra delicately crossed her long arms in front of her.

"On the contrary, I knew you were in the room watching me the entire time, Alix," Sierra announced. My face flushed instantly. I blinked several times hoping some kind of lame excuse would pop into my head.

"Well?" questioned Sierra with a quirky grin. I was confused by her train of thought.

"Well, what?" I answered. She quickly flashed a white pearly smile then turned around in a complete circle.

"Do you approve of what you see?" she seductively asked. Dumbfounded by her question, I nervously stood in silence.

"I asked you a direct question, Agent Becker, and I expect a direct answer," she demanded in an irritated tone.

"Yes! I more than approve of what I see!" I exclaimed. Excitement filled my senses.

"Good, so now that your hormonal issues have been addressed, may we get on with our meeting?" Sierra's smile vanished as she eagerly moved to her briefcase which lay on the table. I knew instantly it was a rhetorical question and thought best just to keep my mouth closed at this point.

"As of now, there are no suspects. Am I correct with that assumption, Alix?" Sierra Montgomery did not make eye contact. I felt a bit awkward knowing Sierra knew of my obvious attraction toward my superior officer.

"Yes," I mumbled with sweaty palms. Sierra continued to glance through her papers.

"We need to jump start this Task Force into a whole new direction. I haven't had a chance to completely examine each and every file. But I can tell you one thing; we're missing a big piece. And we need to find out what that piece is fast before this sadistic killer strikes again. The President is not happy at all on how all this has been handled and that includes the media." Sierra stopped abruptly then looked directly at me. Her beautiful eyes sparkled.

"Did you hear what I said, Alix?" she queried without breaking eye contact.

"Yes, I did, Sierra. I agree with you. There's a definite connection between all the victims including the President's niece, Linda Haley. I'm still working on it. As you already know, Special Agent Harris had been assigned to bring these killings to a halt. We really haven't had enough time…" But before I could finish my thought, Sierra shook her head with disagreement.

"I do not want to hear about not having enough time! This is not a viable excuse when it comes to death! How many more bodies do you need before you can connect the dots? And, I am well aware of Special Agent Harris' transition from White House Aide to her part-time role of Sherlock Holmes." Sierra seemed truly upset by the lack of attention given to this investigation.

"I'm sorry, Alix, I don't mean to dump it all on you. I know you are doing the best you can. It's just…" And before Sierra could finish, her pager vibrated against her waist.

"Will you excuse me?" Instantly, Sierra moved to use the wall phone. Within seconds, her conversation with the unknown party had ended.

"I have to go," she said hurriedly. I stood alone as Sierra raced right past me without any type of explanation for her abrupt departure.

It was more than obvious Sierra Montgomery seemed to be settled with her individuality. Her poise and assertiveness could be interpreted as intimidating, but also refreshing, contrasting to the intrusive and rude demur of Lena Harris. I unequivocally anxiously waited for our next one-on-one encounter; probably more than Sierra would ever realize.

CHAPTER 5

Days ran into nights as I devoted my entire waking hours to the ongoing investigation. The tension I had experienced with Sierra had vanished even though our constant communication remained strictly on a professional level. The entire Task Force was revamped and new faces were given new assignments.

"I don't understand, Alix." Sierra impatiently paced back and forth in front of my desk.

"For each step forward, two steps back," mumbled Sierra.

"Could this investigation somehow be compromised?" she murmured. It had become more and more difficult for me to focus directly on the problems at hand. My attraction to Sierra had grown in leaps and bounds since we first met. I tried desperately to gather my thoughts and grab hold of the slight possibility of an inside snitch.

"It wouldn't be the first time an investigation had been tampered with only to find out years later it was deliberately sabotaged from the very beginning!" I exclaimed.

"I don't feel we need to disclose our suspicions to the rest of the Task Force; especially Harris." Sierra looked worried. There had been rumors regarding Lena's intense dislike for Sierra not only professionally, but also personally.

"I agree with you; it could be anyone at this point, even Lena," I commented. Sierra's eyes met mine and held them fast.

"Do you honestly believe Lena is capable of betraying her own country?" she whispered.

"Could Lena be the leak in the faucet? Yes, I honestly feel she could pull off anything she puts her mind to do. I don't trust Lena Harris in the least. She intentionally takes advantage using her political authority and status of rank." My mind flashed back to that first day with Lena Harris and her unwarranted sexual advances displayed during lunch.

"So, she came on to you?" Sierra's slight smile slipped across her lovely face. I was amazed by her intuitive instincts.

"Yes, she exhibited explicit direction with regards to our relationship. But ever since you came into the picture, she seems to have distanced herself from the entire investigation and thankfully, from me," I explained. Sierra nodded in agreement.

"We agree this is a good thing. Let's keep it that way." Just then my office door sprung open. Lena Harris boldly forged her way inside.

"I just spoke with the President. He wants to know why we haven't caught the killer yet. He had to bury his niece without bringing the prick who mutilated her to justice. What am I suppose to say to him?" Lena threw up her arms. Her voice became loud and boisterous. I remained still as tension mounted in the air.

"We are looking at the entire investigation from a different perspective, as we speak. That's all I can tell you right now. You've read my reports." Sierra refused to back down to Lena's hollow caveats.

"What new angle? How come I wasn't apprised of this? Or do you plan on keeping it a secret?" Her eyes narrowed as she glared at Sierra.

"I am not at liberty to say," replied Sierra with authority.

"Not at liberty! Who on earth do you think you are woman?" Lena shouted. Sierra did not flinch.

"This obvious show of excessive assertiveness is worthless and not appreciated. I am your equal, in rank and position whether you conceivable agree to it or not. This discussion has ended." Lena seemed slightly taken back while Sierra swept her aside.

"Don't you dare walk away from me with that high and mighty attitude of yours!" bellowed Lena.

"I put you down once, Montgomery, and I'll do it again; but this time, you won't be getting back up and that's a promise!" Lena hissed with venom. This unwarranted display of aggression by Lena did not phase nor surprise Sierra.

"I will pretend I didn't hear those browbeating words that came from your brass mouth, Special Agent Harris!" And with nothing left to discuss, Sierra turned on her heel and swiftly exited into the hallway.

I thought for a moment that Lena Harris would explode into pieces as anger and fury seethed from her blood red face. But instead she took a deep breath and mercilessly focused her avenging wrath toward me.

"You *will* tell me what I need to know!" Lena ordered. Her beady dark eyes bored right through me. But before I could respond to Lena's irrational demand, her cell phone chimed a lively tune.

"I'm not through with you, Becker!" Lena hurriedly snatched it from her pocket and stormed out of my office. The sweat on my brow clung tightly against my damp forehead. I thankfully closed the door to be alone.

I began to wonder about the powerful connection between Lena and Sierra. I had a strong feeling these two women had crossed paths at another time and from their display of antagonistic behavior, the battle had been carried throughout the years. My curiosity was more than just tweaked. I had to find out how I fit into this masterful conjectured puzzle while these two powerful and intriguing women battle wits in search of the truth. It would seem I had no choice, but to hold on and brace myself for the rocky ride down an unknown road called fate.

CHAPTER 6

The cold and bitter arctic air swept across the northeast corner of Ohio when we received word from the Toledo Police Department. An anonymous cell phone call had come in which could prove to be vital in solving the stalled murder cases. Sadly, this turbulent news flash included yet one more body added to the growing number on the list.

The three of us rode in total silence for the entire ride. Without any confrontation from Lena, Sierra took hold of the rein and made it to Toledo in record time. The area had already been sealed off by the local police department and bright yellow tape was strung meticulously about the plush wooded area.

"She's over here!" An elderly white haired man anxiously waved his arms back and forth. His long black overcoat flapped open from the wintry mixed wind. Eagerly he stuck his frigid hands back inside the side pockets.

"Ladies, I'm Mel Calldridge. I work with the State Police. A call came through early this morning to the Sheriff's department giving an exact location of where to find a body. We were able to trace the call back to a cell phone. The original owner of the phone said he lost it about a week ago, but never got around to calling the provider about the missing phone. So, we don't have much to go on by way of tracking who really made the call. Do you think it's your guy who did the dirty work?" The tall oversized gentlemen shivered.

The damp ground sucked hungrily at our boots making it difficult to walk. Dried bushes and dead limbs grabbed at our clothes as the three of us tried to move about the crime scene. Mud oozed from under my feet as I left deep impressions in the sinking mass. The smell of rotted wood drifted in the crisp air. I looked around hastily wondering how much of the area had actually been searched for evidence. It must have rained at one time to saturate the sodden ground that had been covered by a recent fresh snow. But even with the cold brisk weather, the stench of death hung heavy leaving me slightly dizzy. Mother Nature, in all of its beauty, had not been good to her. The nude crumpled and slashed female body lay haphazardly against a large oak tree. Small pieces of flesh were missing from her skull. A dark gaping hole, that once was an eye, stared blindly out to nowhere. Her corpse had been viscously violated. Tiny parasites were busily eating their way through the discolored skin. Sierra and Lena immediately began to examine the remains. Within minutes Sierra had photographed the body from every possible angle.

"Alix, hand me a brown vial. I want to snag a couple of these insects for the lab. It will give us the actual time of death." I reached inside the crime lab kit. Lena then scooped up the crawling creatures.

"You ladies seem to have everything under control. I will leave you to your investigation." Mel Calldridge tipped his head slightly to the side.

"And if we need to contact you at a later date?" questioned Lena.

"Here's my number. You can reach me day or night." He reluctantly jiggled a bent business card out of his inside pocket.

"Oh, by the way, I didn't catch any of your names?" Calldridge stood silent for a moment.

"We didn't throw them. We're the FBI and that's all *you* need to know! Thanks for your limited amount of help, Kal." Lena's eyes never left the dead body.

"The name's Mel Calldridge! Women!" he mumbled under his breath as in left in a huff. Sierra continued to photograph the surrounding area throughout the murder scene. I took several notes on the placement and position of the body, along with the obvious physical signs of trauma and current weather conditions.

"There's someone in a hooded jacket watching us from behind those trees about 500 hundred yards to the left," stated Sierra with grave concern. For a brief moment I stood frozen in my tracks.

"Probably another officer in blue taking a peak," muttered Lena.

"Nope, hate to disappoint you, Lena, but this person has a rifle and is aiming it straight at us." Suddenly, Sierra dropped her camera then knocked me heavily to the ground. The impact was hard and painful. Just then the sound of whizzing bullets passed directly above our heads.

"This guy is going to be sorry when I get through with him," shouted Lena. She immediately withdrew her Beretta and began to return fire.

"Are you okay, Alix?" Sierra urgently patted me down to make sure I was not hit by any stray bullets.

"I'm fine, Sierra," I replied while thoroughly enjoying the ravenous examination.

"Well, whoever it was took off," yelled Lena. Sierra immediately used her telephoto lens to search the area

"You're right, he's gone." Sierra and I stood up and tried to brush off some of the heavy mud that stuck to our faded jeans.

"I guess there's no question about it, now," announced Lena.

"The female victim definitely has the same MO as the others, but this time we had a real live gun toting visitor. This case just keeps getting better and better," commented Lena sarcastically.

"Let's finish up and get out of here," replied Sierra.

The silent ride back was more than uncomfortable. Once again, not one of us spoke a single word. By now the freezing rain had turned to heavy solid flakes. The wipers swiftly removed them as fast as they fell. Finally, I could stand it no more and broke the tensioned atmosphere.

"I have this dreadful feeling the guy we're looking for was the one who shot at us." I longed for an intelligent conversation. Lena rolled her eyes and grunted.

"You think? Now I know why you're an agent!" Sarcasm seeped through her lips. Sierra's eyes narrowed.

"Lena, that remark was uncalled for and most unprofessional. Did you ever think that maybe Alix was trying to lighten the load and get rid of the baggage *someone* seems to be carrying around during this investigation?" retorted Sierra in my defense.

"And what is that suppose to mean? I didn't ask for you or your inefficient help! I was handling this bundling investigation just fine until you stuck your nose in it!" exclaimed Lena. The snow on the road had turned to ice as the temperature began to dip below freezing.

"Okay, I didn't mean to start a war between the two of you. It's just that…that we all have to work with one another so why not make the best of it?" I tried to ease the anxiety which had escalated between the two hot headed females.

"Oh, you didn't start a war, Alix; it's been here the entire time." Sierra looked the other way.

"Hmmm…it's the first thing we actually agree on, eh, Sierra?" Lena chuckled then muttered something under her breath. I led out a deep sigh and thought best to keep my mouth closed for the remainder of the trip. Sierra, in turn, glanced my way and winked. Immediately, my face blushed with embarrassment while excitement filled my senses. I felt like a school girl with her first crush. I thought for a second perhaps Sierra may have a personal interest in me. But, like anything else, only time would tell.

I felt a bit tired when we finally arrived at the Cleveland Division. Our expertise assessment and the evidence the three of us had gathered were considered crucial and essential in order to solve the multiple murders.

Lena Harris disappeared after her brief conversation with the Agent in Charge. I, on the other hand, lingered about hoping to bump into Sierra.

"Sierra, do you mind if I walk out with you?" I asked nonchalantly. Her quick step instantly stopped.

"I want to thank you, well, thank you for what you did today. If you hadn't pushed me out of the direct line of fire, who knows, I could be down in a drawer inside the morgue right now." As I gazed into her intense, yet gentle eyes, I felt her reaching out to me. Without saying a word, she gently touched my cheek with her delicate fingertip. I immediately resisted the overwhelming urge to kiss her. I felt drawn in by her magnetic aura.

"It's not a big deal," she replied quickly removing her hand away from my face. She cleared her throat and casually looked away.

"We need to be extremely careful, Alix. Whoever that was this afternoon will probably try again. We're all in danger." Sierra began to walk towards the parking garage. I hurried to stay by her side.

"I'm in total agreement with you, Sierra." As we parted to each vehicle, Sierra stopped briefly and faced me.

"My hotel is just down the road. Would you like to join me for a late dinner?" she asked unexpectedly. I was dumbstruck for a moment. She took my lack of response as rejection.

"I didn't mean to put you in an awkward position." She jingled her keys then turned to leave. Fearing her retreat, I hurriedly accepted the unforeseen invitation.

"I would love to!" I insisted in a loud clear voice. Her smile warmed my heart.

"Okay, follow me!" My heart skipped a beat at the thought of spending time "off the clock" with this vibrant woman. Within minutes Sierra and I arrived at the Crown Regency Hotel.

The hotel restaurant was cozy, and even better yet, almost empty. A roaring fireplace radiated streams of warmth across the exquisite dining area. We both ordered a light sandwich due to the lateness of the hour. I felt at ease but a bit anxious with Sierra. I was eager to learn all I could during our uninterrupted time together.

"Why do you and Harris bump heads so much, if I may be so bold to ask?" I threw out this tender subject for open conversation. Sierra immediately stopped chewing her food then delicately wiped her thin luscious lips.

"I'm impressed, Alix, at your keen sense of observation. I was sure the façade remained solid…" I knew in an instant she was toying with me, but I didn't mind at all. In fact, I rather enjoyed her undivided attention.

"You deserve truth and the truth you shall hear." Sierra continued to eat. We were silent as we finished our informal dinner.

"I was working for the CIA as an undercover operative. We were stationed at the Al Assad military air base near Baghdad. I was tracking an informer from the Abdu Ahushad terrorist group. The informant's name was Rahul Bahhuld. So for over a year, I had to live as one of the members inside with Ahushad and the others. We originally suspected Bahhuld of selling United States military secrets to the Iraqis but this was never confirmed. Strangely enough, it was his infiltration within the Iraqi government which initiated a code red here with the U.S. Chief of Defense. In the meantime, I found out that Rahul had his own agenda. He hated the Iraqi government for giving in to the U.S. and in turn loathed the U.S. for their intense military intervention. I was able to earn Rahul's confidence and in a strange sense of the word we had actually become what you might call comrades. But within that short period of time, the mission had taken a major turn for the worse. My new orders were to immediately eliminate Rahul along with the entire terrorist group." Sierra took a sip of cool water from her sweating glass.

"You must understand, Alix, I became an intricate part within the lives of these people. They weren't all soldiers; there were many women and children too. I had great difficulty accepting the realization that even the children would have to die for a cause they did not understand." Sierra appeared to be upset.

"It was my hesitancy and resentment towards our government that brought Lena Harris into the picture. Lena and her command of five soldiers had been sent in to assist me, or should I say to make sure the entire terrorist group would be eliminated. We overtook Rahul and his group out in the middle of the Montobe desert by surprise. I will never forget that day as long as I live. Lena ordered the men to be separated from women and children. She had them lined up and then executed by firing squad. I tried desperately to reason with her regarding the lives of innocent women and children. Lena would hear nothing of it. I even suggested turning them in to the Iraqi government but..." Sierra's eyes glazed over as her mind flashed back in time.

"I watched in horror as Lena commanded her men to fire round after round into the helpless women and children while they huddled together and prayed. Their blood saturated the dry sandy ground." Tears filled Sierra's sorrowful eyes.

"Because of my extreme concern regarding the families of the terrorists, Lena accused me of treason. I came back to the States and stood trial. Luckily, the charges were dropped and I left the CIA to work with the FBI." Sierra quickly looked away.

"What happened to Rahul?" I asked softly

"I heard the interrogation lasted five minutes. Lena slit his throat." Sierra shrugged her sagging shoulders.

"Alix, don't misunderstand me. What this man did or tried to accomplish was immoral, unethical and murderous. His ludicrous attempts at trying to create a freedom, at the cost of other people's lives, were more than just insane. Rahul needed to be stopped. But I just can't get it out of mind the useless slaughter of innocent children..." Sierra's voice trailed off into silence. I suddenly felt this urgent need to comfort her.

"Am I making any sense at all?" whispered Sierra.

"Yes, you are Sierra." I nodded in agreement.

"Lena Harris is a ruthless and heartless murderer. She kills for the sake of killing." Sierra looked up just in time as the server reappeared.

"Can I get you two ladies anything else this evening?" she asked politely. Her ponytail swished back and forth behind her young looking face.

"No, thank you," replied Sierra. Without saying another word, Sierra and I got up to leave. As we approached my parked car, Sierra suddenly leaned in and kissed me briefly on my lips. Butterflies raced inside while hidden urges streamed forth with gusto.

"Please Alix, you must be careful. Lena is a very dangerous woman," warned Sierra. Sierra lightly squeezed my arm then quietly headed toward the staircase leading to her hotel suite.

I stood alone for a moment inside the cold vacated parking garage and watched Sierra walk away. The chill of the night air made me shiver. My thoughts swirled and collided with my escalating attraction to Sierra and her ominous words of warning.

This had been the second time I was forewarned of Lena Harris' violent tendencies. My friend, Sandy Lewis, trembled at the very thought of this evil woman. And now, an ex-CIA agent, Sierra Montgomery, revealed her deepest secrets surrounding the destructive powers which Lena Harris held in the palm of her hand. My confusion intensified as I tried desperately to connect this vital information to the serial killer investigations. Then suddenly my mind switched gears and my thoughts lingered on the sudden kiss from Sierra. It was more than welcomed and I eagerly waited to spend more time with this special woman even as the unsolved murders inched themselves ahead.

CHAPTER 7

The results of the evidence found at the last crime scene in Toledo had been analyzed. A positive identification had been made through dental records, but the name was being held back from the media. Don Fielding, Agent in Charge, requested a short meeting with Sierra and me.

"Ladies, please have a seat." With that invitation both Sierra and I sat down in the cushiony chairs which sat adjacent to the front of his disorderly desk.

"I called you both in to inform you that Special Agent Harris has been called back to Washington D.C. This leaves you, Special Agent Montgomery to oversee the entire Task Force and its members. Agent Becker, you are to assist Special Agent Montgomery in any way possible. That means we are expecting miracles, ladies. Let's face it. I've got not only the media crawling up my ass, but higher ups in Washington and they are making my life a living nightmare!" Frustration pulled across his pudgy face. Fielding clenched his teeth before letting out a huge sigh.

"My wife says I'm going to give myself a heart attack one of these days. I think she may be right." Don Fielding opened his side drawer and pulled out a huge container of Tums. Grabbing several at once he tossed them into his mouth and began to chew vigorously.

"Ladies, I know I don't have to tell you how important it is to solve these murder cases. We have had a bit of bad luck. Sometimes I wonder if maybe information isn't somehow…anyway, I'd appreciate anything you can do right now to make my life easier." Suddenly, Fielding stood up signaling the end of the meeting. Sierra and I left without saying a word.

"You're not surprised Lena is gone, are you?" I questioned Sierra as we slowly walked down the hall together.

"No. And, between you and me, she didn't go back to Washington. She's still here, Alix. She's watching and waiting." Sierra abruptly went into her office alone. Again, I felt confused and agitated at the same time. A piece was missing to this mysterious puzzle. As I sat behind my own disorganized desk, I tried to meticulously review each and every bit of information that had been fed to me during my conversations with Sandy Lewis and Sierra Montgomery.

"Are you lost in deep thought?" Sierra surprisingly popped her head inside my office.

"What is it?" I asked with a huge smile plastered across my face.

"Come on; we're going to take a ride," replied Sierra. Within minutes of leaving the Bureau, Sierra filled me in on the details regarding the interview we were to conduct with Commissioner Robert Lansing.

Commissioner Lansing's mansion was more than just elite. An elegant gothic moor chandelier hung majestically from the enormous high ceiling. The hallway, filled with exquisite and antique furniture, set the scene for a postmodern décor. Intrigued by its elaborate beauty and architectural design, Sierra and I walked slowly ingesting its magnificence. For a brief moment, I stood in awe at the enormous study which had been meticulously hand picked and stacked with a fine prestigious collection of old historical law books.

"Afternoon Commissioner." Sierra politely greeted the sorrowful politician.

"Sir," I added with a slight nod.

"Good afternoon, Special Agent Montgomery and Agent Becker. Please sit down. Would you like a cup of hot tea or coffee?" The Commissioner motioned to the overstuffed love seat, which sat close against the sidewall of the study. From the opposite side of the room entered a tall elderly gentleman dressed in a black suit. His shapely bowtie could barely be seen as it blended perfectly into the creases of the dark colored shirt. He skillfully balanced a large oval silver tray with several china teacups, a small porcelain teapot, and a unique coffee urn with all the accompanying condiments.

"Hot tea or coffee, maaam?" drawled the aging gent. His silver hair shined in the dim lights illuminating from the front of the study. With half closed eyes, he silently gazed past Sierra and waited for an answer.

"Hot tea would be fine. Thank you." Sierra flashed a quick grin.

"And for you, hot tea or coffee, maam?" The attendant faced me with deliberate movements, yet seemed to be aloof.

"Hot tea, thank you," I murmured. As the elderly man set down the tray to pour our tea, the Commissioner busily lit the fire in the old stone fireplace. Within minutes, the roaring hot flames evaporated the dampness leaving only warmth to fill its place.

Commissioner Lansing leaned gently against the leathery surface of the high back chair that sat mightily behind an enormous mahogany desk. With his head slightly down and fingers intertwined, he seemed to be oblivious to our presence.

"Charles?" softly spoke the Commissioner.

"Yes, sir?" answered the old man.

"Please hold all my calls. I do not want to be disturbed unless it is an emergency. And I mean an emergency." He looked across the room at the two of us. His face was consumed with grief. His eyes glistened sadly against the radiating ambers from the burning fire.

"Yes, sir." The elderly chap bowed slightly. Sierra waited until the door of the study had closed before she began to speak.

"First, Commissioner Lansing, let me extend our deepest sympathy on the loss of your daughter.

"Bob," he said without feeling.

"Excuse me, sir?" Sierra glanced at me with a puzzled expression.

"Call me Bob." Commissioner Lansing heaved a tremendous sigh.

"Alright, Bob. We, at the FBI, understand this is an extremely difficult time in your life and with your help, we would like to, as quickly as possible, apprehend the person who committed this violence against your daughter and others." Sierra cleared her throat.

"It would seem the FBI isn't, or should I say, may not be taking these murders too seriously!" Bob swiveled about to face the warming fire. His words stung deep. Within a moment he continued on in a trembling voice.

"My daughter, she was a good woman; a good mother and a good wife. She never hurt anyone. In fact, she went out of her way to help others. She volunteered her time and services on so many occasions. She was involved in many worthwhile projects. She helped the homeless, the elderly, volunteered time at wayward houses for abused women, raised money for orphanages! Hell, she even worked for me part-time…" His voice trailed off into an unsettling silence.

"So many things, so much time and energy she constantly gave of herself, all for the sake of what, to be murdered by some freak of nature? Who gave him the right to take her life? Who gave him the right to take away my daughter from me; a mother from her children and a wife from her husband? Who? Tell me, who gave him the ultimate right to play God?" Suddenly, he swung himself around and immediately rose from his chair. His eyes were filled with rage. He gritted his teeth in anguished despair. Sierra stood up as if she was about to leave, but instead she gingerly took a step toward Commissioner Lansing.

"Why? Oh, why did it have to be my daughter?" The Commissioner unexpectedly collapsed and began to sob in hopeless desperation.

"Commissioner Lansing, I mean, Bob. We appreciate the fact you allowed us to enter your home. Again, please accept our sympathy. We'll see ourselves out." The Commissioner did not respond nor did he budge from the high back chair. Neither one of us said a word. An eerie emptiness suddenly filled the endless hallway as we closed the front door.

Our instructions to interview Commissioner Robert Lansing had not been carried out. Questioning him now, in his delicate state of mind, could be of no use to us or to him. The shock of losing his daughter seemed too much for the Commissioner to bear, as it would be to anyone who had lost a loved one to such a horrible and violent death. Sierra remained quiet while we sat together inside the debriefing room. Her shapely thigh rested lightly against mine. I couldn't help but to gaze into her beautiful eyes that were filled with determination. It became a challenge to submerge my exploding emotions that I held deep inside.

"Alix…" is all she said before the untimely interruption. Her cell phone chimed loudly.

"This is Special Agent Montgomery," she answered. Her smooth forehead wrinkled with concern as she nodded several times without saying a word.

"Yes, we're on it." She clicked her phone closed.

"This might be it, our luck perhaps is changing for the better!" she exclaimed.

"Let's go, I'll fill you in while I drive." Without hesitation, Sierra and I eagerly set out hoping to find the missing piece of what seemed to be a never ending puzzle.

CHAPTER 8

The drive to San Panzel Penitentiary would have been potentially long and boring except for the wonderful fact I was alone, again, with Sierra. Our conversation focused on the two inmates who just might provide a useable slice of tangible evidence.

We entered the enormous brown and red brick building through the steel metal front doors. Electric wired fencing surrounded the entire perimeter of the prison broadcasting to those inside that there was no chance to escape. The interrogation cell held a sour smell since it had recently been painted a dull shade of flat gray. An oblong two-way mirror edged itself out across the room.

"If I can be of further assistance to either of you lovely ladies, please, just give me a holler!" Warden Larry Holden was overly generous as he escorted us personally inside. Within minutes, the two prisoners hobbled in wearing bright orange jumpsuits and shiny steel handcuffs. Rap sheets on each of these men revealed long-term prison sentences including convictions for assault with a deadly weapon and armed robbery.

"Whoopee! Hey Daryl, whatcha' think my man?" Curtis Jackson, the shorter of the two men, had a quirky grin plastered across his pot-marked face. His thin greasy hair stuck to his sweating scalp. Several of his front teeth were missing leaving a gaping dark hole as he tried to smile. Daryl Thorton, his cellmate and partner in crime, was much taller and older. His boyish features and frail appearance made it hard to believe he could be a threat to anyone. Both men reeked of musty sweat.

"Hell, Curtis, they're not here for our manly pleasure!" As Daryl Thorton spoke, a small trickle of snot slowly leaked down from his nostril.

"Sit down and shut your mouths! Don't speak unless you're spoken to, assholes!" The prison guard roughly shoved Curtis and Daryl toward the seats directly across from us.

"Let me know if this pile of crap gives you any trouble!" The guard tipped his hat and headed out the door. Sierra glanced my way before she began the interview.

"Daryl J. Thorton and Curtis A. Jackson." Sierra stated their names in a firm voice as she made direct eye contact with each one of them.

"I am Special Agent Montgomery and this is Agent Becker. We are here to ask you two gentlemen a few questions." Sierra paused a second, but was quickly cut off.

"Hey, hey, what's so special about you? Huh?" Curtis Jackson slurred his words then snorted like a pig. Daryl eyed Sierra slyly up and down.

"She's not special, Curtis. She bleeds like the rest of them pigs," chuckled Daryl. I leaned back into my chair and instantly came to the conclusion this was going to be a major waste of our valuable time.

"Dang Daryl! You're nothin' but a shiny ladies man!" Curtis grunted again.

"Gentlemen, Agent Becker and I would like to ask you a few questions regarding a discussion you two had with another inmate, Mr. James Rascliffe." Sierra seemed to be getting no where fast.

"Mr. James Rascliffe!" mimicked Curtis Jackson in a high whimsical tone.

"Hell, lady, his name's Jimmy Boy," spat Daryl Thorton.

"Looky here, Curtis, I got me a boner!" Daryl Thorton grabbed at his crouch with both cuffed hands. Not impressed or shocked by his gestures, Sierra pressed on.

"Gentlemen, if I may have your attention please." Sierra sighed as if her patience was beginning to wear thin.

"Geez, Daryl! You get a boner just lookin' at the ugly guards, man!" Both prisoners burst out laughing. I had just about enough when Sierra unexpectedly slammed her hand flat down on the table. Surprised by this display of aggression, both men jumped back a bit and shut their mouths.

"Look, I'm tired of being polite! Either you answer the questions or I have the guard return you to your cells." Sierra spoke through gritted teeth. The small veins along the side of her head expanded as they neared her temples.

"Do you two," Sierra cleared her throat, "gentlemen think you can stay composed and focused long enough to answer me?" Her lips were drawn tight. Curtis wiped the snot from his lip with the back of his dirty hand while Daryl sneered at Sierra's insistence.

"Good. I am glad we finally understand one another. Now, if you don't mind, please tell us about the conversation you had with an inmate by the name of Jimmy Boy." Sierra showed no signs of backing down.

"Okay, Daryl here chummed up with this feller, Jimmy Boy, who was a braggin' about the women he done and cut up. You know the important ones?" Curtis picked at his right nostril with his index finger. Sierra and I glanced at one another.

"Daryl, is this true? What exactly did Jimmy Boy say to you?" Sierra moved forward in her seat. I eagerly waited to jot down something of value.

"Daryl?" pushed Sierra.

"I don't member all that was said. You got a big mouth Curtis!" Daryl Thorton spat, once again, on the ground just inches from my shoe.

"I do remember one thing; he said he hated carpet munchers!" Daryl's left nostril twitched. His sheepish grin had become overly annoying.

"You know all about them carpet munchers; pussy eatin' pussy." Once again, the two jail birds loudly cackled together. Sierra briefly closed her eyes and exhaled.

"The correct term is lesbian. Are you saying that one of the victims was a lesbian?" Daryl leaned forward in his seat to respond.

"I'm just repeating what Jimmy Boy said. Why don't you go ask him if he cut the pussy eater?" Curtis rocked in his chair and snickered.

"Pussy eater! Pussy eater!" chanted Curtis.

"Is there anything else you two gentlemen can tell us?" I asked. Daryl Thorton stared hard at Sierra.

"What's in it for Curtis and me?" Sierra knew Daryl was holding back.

"Not a single thing. You're both convicted felons each serving a long prison sentence; plain and simple. I think we're finished here Special Agent Montgomery." I began to rise from the table.

"Wait! He got paid." blurted out Curtis. Daryl immediately nudged Curtis in the ribs.

"Are you saying someone paid Jimmy Boy to commit these murders?" Sierra raised her eyebrows. Curtis Jackson looked worried. Daryl shook his head in disbelieve.

"I guess that's what I'm sayin'," mumbled Curtis with his head hung low.

"Did Jimmy Boy perhaps mention a name?" pressed Sierra. Daryl's chest swelled and decided to answer this time.

"You'll have to ask Jimmy Boy yourself. We're done talkin'." Daryl threw Curtis a dirty look. Both prisoners remained quiet. Curtis Jackson shifted uneasily in his seat. He seemed to be a bit nervous by the continuous glares from Daryl Thorton. The guard was summoned and the two men were promptly returned to their jail cells.

"So what do you think, Alix?" asked Sierra as we rode back to the city.

"I have a gut feeling the two of them were telling the truth. I think we need to interview this guy, Jimmy Boy," I replied in all honesty. Sierra nodded in agreement.

"But what makes you so sure he'll tell us anything?" questioned Sierra.

"I'm not sure at all. But why would he deny it especially since he got paid a hefty sum? It sounds to me like he's a bragger. Maybe he feels if he tells his story no one on the inside will bother to mess with him." I was just surmising and trying to convince, not only Sierra, but myself.

"You're optimism truly amazes me, Alix." I could see her smiling inside the dark car. Without an invitation, I moved closer to Sierra. Anxiously, I rested my hand gently on Sierra's shapely thigh. She instantly responded by holding my warm hand. We drove in silence the remainder of the way both lost in our own individual thoughts. As we drew near to the FBI building, I moved back across to the passenger seat. I had to resist the overwhelming temptation to embrace Sierra.

"Alix, I think we need to talk about a very important personal issue." Sierra's serious voice startled me. But before she could say another word, both of our pagers vibrated simultaneously.

SAN PANZEL PRISON: CURTIS JACKSON AND DARYL THORTON—FOUND STABBED TO DEATH IN CELL BLOCK D.

Sierra and I, shocked by the news, immediately looked at one another. Could it be possible Curtis Jackson and Daryl Thorton had been telling the truth? Did our visit to the prison somehow inadvertently sign their death warrants? Without any official directive, Sierra and I decided to head back, but this time for an unannounced visit to San Panzel Penitentiary.

CHAPTER 9

The drive back to San Panzel was fast and furious. Sierra exceeded the speed limit several times breaking record time. The night shift was unappreciative of the fact our immediate need to speak to one of the prisoners. It was now well past 1 a.m. and all cells had been locked down for the night hours ago.

They called him "Cutter Jim, aka Jimmy Boy," but his registered birth name read James Rascliffe. His nickname preceded him as we reviewed his rap sheet with interest. James Rascliffe was serving at least a 25-year stitch for attempted murder and aggravated assault with a deadly weapon (knife), among many other minor criminal charges.

Rascliffe stood roughly about 5' 9" with a modest medium build. His shaved head and thick-framed glasses gave you the impression that at one time in his life, he might have been considered studious. His long pointed nose offset his narrow squared jaw while his scruffy face gave way to his untrusting beady eyes. The bright orange short sleeve prison uniform was dirty and wrinkled. It pulled tightly across his odd shaped body. Rascliffe sat with his hands cuffed behind his back which forced him to lean forward. He was not a happy man.

"Mr. Rascliffe. This is Agent Becker and I am Special Agent Montgomery. May I call you James?" Sierra spoke with a firm yet interested voice.

"No, you may not! My name's Jimmy Boy. There is no Mr. Rascliffe!" he answered sarcastically.

"Jimmy Boy, it is then. I would like to ask you a few questions…" Rudely enough, Sierra was cut off in mid-sentence.

"Look bitch, I'm not talking to you!" Rascliffe vehemently spat on the ground. Sierra exhaled a huge and tiresome sigh. Her patience had worn thin from the previous interview with Curtis and Daryl. It had been an exceptionally long day.

"Due to the lateness of the hour, I would like to make this interview quick. You could make it easier on yourself by cooperating or…?" Sierra left her sentence unfinished. She sat staring at him, eye to eye, each one of them waiting for the other to back down. Sierra's determination won out. James Rascliffe sniffed and spat, again. A huge wad of phlegm plopped near my shoe.

"I know you talked with those two losers Jackson and Thorton. I would think you two would have at least one brain between your vaginal areas and realize that they were imbeciles!" He sniffed again and looked down at the table. Sierra forged ahead.

"So, what you're saying Mr. Rascliffe…" Sierra, once again, had been cut off before getting the chance to finish her question.

"Call me Jimmy Boy!" He sneered at Sierra.

"Jimmy Boy, what you are saying is that the information provided by Curtis Jackson and Daryl Thorton was not factual. If that was the case, they gave up their lives for a pack of lies. Wouldn't you say, Jimmy Boy?" Sierra straightened her papers on the small table.

"Those two bastards hated me. They were pissed off at the fact I turned them in for stealing silverware from the chow line. So they lied!" Rascliffe shook his head in anger.

"It was said you were paid a large sum of money to mutilate and kill targeted women. And according to your bank records, it seems you became a wealthy man overnight. You're looking at serving at least the next 25 years in prison. You won't be spending any of that hard earned cash for a very long time, if at all. I need to know who paid you. You can make this easy or you can make this hard; it's your decision." Sierra sat back in her chair. Her warm leg lightly brushed up against mine. James Rascliffe watched us with immense curiosity. He licked his lips several times. After long moments of silence, Rascliffe decided to negotiate.

"What's in it for me?" mumbled Rascliffe.

"Yeah, what's in it for me?" he repeated with a smart-ass smirk. He wriggled his hands inside the tight fitted cuffs.

"What's in it for you? Well, how about the fact you helped put a high profiled murderer behind bars?" answered Sierra.

"Who said she was high profiled?" Unexpectedly, James Rascliffe was beginning to sweat. Small beads of perspiration formed along the top of his forehead.

"Now, come on, Jimmy Boy, you think a small time hood like you would agree to do such atrocities for a couple hundred bucks? No way, Jimmy Boy! We know you received at least a half a million in cash to cut up those women and dump them. Give me a break! So, who would have that kind of money?" Sierra closed the manila folder and folded her hands on top of the table.

"Now that we know your contact was female, who is she, James? I need a name, now!" Sierra's voice rose with authority. Jimmy Boy was not intimidated by Sierra's looming posture. He grunted a sly response.

"Like I said before, what's in it for me?" Rascliffe's beady dark eyes danced back and forth between the two of us.

"I'll see what I can do for you, but first we need the information." Sierra was determined and persistent.

"Damn, woman! It's Jimmy Boy! Jimmy Boy's the name and cutin' women is my game!" Rascliffe squealed with delight at the thought of being witty and in control. Sierra jumped on his mistake.

"So you admit you did cut and murder those innocent women?" Sierra eagerly sat forward.

"Innocent! You don't know nothin' lady and I didn't admit to no such thing." Rascliffe sniffed then licked his dry, cracked lips.

"This game is over, Jimmy Boy, a name, now." Sierra folded her arms. James Rascliffe sneered. His top lip quivered as his hot tempered blood raced aimlessly into his bulging temples.

It took only a brief second for Rascliffe to unexpectedly lurch forward at Sierra. But luckily his handcuffs held him intact. Hate poured from Rascliffe's constricted eyes as he hissed unrecognizable words. Sierra sat firm and never flinched a muscle. I, on the other hand, instantly stood up and went to draw for my weapon.

"Your girl's got an itchy finger," muttered Rascliffe. Sierra glanced my way and I slowly sat back down.

"Now that you just about confessed to the fact you did kill those women, James Rascliffe, give me a name or I'll have them fry your pathetic ass faster than you can wipe it!" It was Sierra's turn and she was right up in his face. James, the conventional criminal he was, knew full well Sierra meant what she said, but gave little credence to her over zealous threat, and had no intention of backing down.

"You stupid bitch! You really think she gave me her name?" He forced a hearty laugh then shifted uncomfortably in his seat.

"We have records stating you used a pay phone on the corner of 72nd and St. Clair. Is that how you received your instructions, Jimmy Boy?" Sierra shoved the lined piece of paper in front of him. Rascliffe sniffed his leaky nose and remained quiet for a moment.

"You must think I some dumb mother…" It was Sierra's turn as she cut into his vulgar words.

"No, on the contrary, we think you're a smart man, Jimmy Boy. We know you'll give us the information." Rascliffe lowered his head finally in defeat. His balding scalp glistened with sweat.

"I came home to my apartment one day and found a plain white envelope shoved under my door. I opened it up and there was a note. It said I could make a shit load of money. If I decided to take the job, instructions would be given to me over the phone. So, I waited for the call." Rascliffe spoke softly.

"How long ago was this?" questioned Sierra.

"Over a year ago." James Rascliffe was an evil and vial man.

"What age would you guess this woman to be by the sound of her voice?" Sierra pressed on.

"Now I'm a voice expert?" taunted Rascliffe.

"Like I mentioned before, Jimmy, you seem to be a relatively intellectual man," fibbed Sierra.

"Look agent lady, I'm not falling for your psycho analyzing bull crap!" Rascliffe suddenly exploded flashing his nicotine stained teeth. Sierra gave me a brief nod indicating the interview was over. We retrieved about as much information as we were going to get from James Rascliffe. I motioned for the guard to open the cell door.

"Let's go you filthy maggot! I'll be more than happy to escort his royalty back to his cozy palace." The muscular guard grabbed Rascliffe roughly by the arms lifting him up in the air. Rascliffe squealed in pain. As the guard leaned in close, he mumbled something that only Rascliffe could possibly hear. Rascliffe frantically tried to break free from the guard's unbreakable hold. We could still hear the piercing screams echo through the empty prison halls as we made our way outside. No doubt they came from James Rascliffe, aka, Jimmy Boy.

CHAPTER 10

Sierra called a special meeting of the Task Force to review the information retrieved from the inmates at San Panzel. Overnight word had leaked out from the prison to the media on the stabbing death of two convicted criminals and their weak connection to the investigation. This only reiterated the lack of movement within the FBI. But even with all the bad publicity, I still couldn't shake the feeling that Lena was involved somehow and connected to this whole mess.

"Sierra, don't you think it's rather strange that Lena has not tried to contact either one of us?" I waited patiently for her answer. She looked up from her reading.

"Well, no. I know she wouldn't bother to call me and you? The only reason she would want to talk with you, Alix, is to...well..." My face blushed innocently and I felt a little flattered.

"The fact of the matter still remains, if this investigation was a high enough priority to send a Presidential aide in the first place, why in the world would that person suddenly be called back to Washington D.C.?" I tried not to sound so insistent and become a pest with my theory. Sierra sat studying the reports at the long table. The briefing room felt unusually frigid. A slight chill ran down my spine. We both remained silent for a moment.

"I don't think she ever left, Alix. I still think here, like I said before, watching and waiting to see what kind of progress we make with the investigation." Sierra's train of thought was more than just feasible.

"I totally agree with you, Sierra. In fact, I have this gut feeling Lena has a definite involvement with the killings. And I also think she knew the President's niece." I proudly sat down next to Sierra. She looked quite surprised by my thorough intuitive insight.

"Wow, I'm impressed!" exclaimed Sierra with a small smile drawn across her lovely face. Suddenly, I had an overwhelming urge, once again, to kiss her soft lips. Without hesitation I leaned in and gently pressed my eager lips against hers. Excitement roared through my body overloading my senses. Within a second, Sierra abruptly pulled back and broke the magical spell.

"I am so sorry, Sierra. I…I don't know what came over me!" My face was flushed from pure ecstasy. It was more than obvious I wanted to be with this woman. Sierra, on the other hand, cleared her throat and went right back to studying the reports ignoring our brief personal contact. Embarrassment was not well worn especially now, after my episode of flaunting. I felt extremely uncomfortable. I tried desperately to focus on work. Sierra seemed to be deep in thought. It was no use, though; I needed to clear the air between us.

"Sierra, this has been extremely awkward for me…" But before I could finish my sentence, Sierra quickly moved against me and encircled my body with her muscular arms. She roughly grabbed at my short brown hair tugging my head back to nuzzle hungrily at my open neck. My hands feverishly moved about Sierra's luscious body as we thrashed together as one. Within minutes we both frantically had shed our clothes and succumbed willingly to our erotic needs and desires, right in the middle, on the debriefing room floor.

"Special Agent Montgomery, line 5…Special Agent Montgomery, line 5," boomed a voice from above. Sierra urgently pushed my naked body aside and scrambled for the house phone. With her hair a mess and minus her clothes, Sierra stopped to regain her composure before answering the call.

"This is Special Agent Montgomery," she responded professionally. I gazed heavenly upon her sexy glistened body while she urgently pointed to her blouse and pants thrown across the floor. I giggled to myself and began to collect her belongings.

"Yes, sir, a full report will be ready to be sent to the President by late afternoon. Agent Becker and I were just about finished…" Sierra covered her mouth and tried to keep a straight face. Her voluptuous breasts bounced slightly.

"I will, sir." Sierra quickly hung up the phone. Our sexual interlude had lasted no longer than a half hour. But it was one of the most fulfilling sensual encounters I had ever experienced. I could no longer deny the love that was growing inside for this wonderful woman.

We hurriedly picked up our garments and dressed without a word. I couldn't help but to stare at her perfectly shaped body. She, too, could not keep her wandering eyes off me.

"Okay, Alix, I agree with you." Sierra was slipping back on her shoes. For a moment, I was a bit confused.

"Your thoughts on Lena's involvement with the murder victims," responded Sierra a little out of breath. By now the two of us were completely dressed and ready to leave.

"You do?" I was amazed at her concurrence to my unsupported accusations.

"I told you before…I *know* the real Lena Harris. She's connected to this whole mess somehow and is hiding under the auspice of the President." The FBI offices and corridors had thinned out. Sierra sealed the highly confidential package and had it expressed to the President's advisor.

"Something else bothers me," I said out loud. Sierra was behind her desk typing rapidly on her keyboard.

"There are unaccountable hours prior to the disappearance of each victim. Linda Haley, the President's niece, was scheduled to attend an important political lesbian/gay rally. She wouldn't dare miss such an important event; but she did. Linda's neighbor states he saw her with a woman, mid-thirties, shoulder length hair, etc. etc." I read the remainder of the description of the unknown woman to myself. Then, suddenly, it hit me!

"I know this may be a long shot, Sierra, but what if we were to question the neighbor again and this time show him a picture of Lena!" Sierra abruptly stopped working.

"Are you saying Lena was having an affair with the President's niece?" Sierra's mouth dropped open.

"Why not? Lena's sexually active record precedes her according to a close acquaintance." My mind instantly darted to Sandy.

"I'm sure she had ample time to socialize with Linda Haley at the White House," replied Sierra. Maybe I was just grasping at straws.

"Why kill her, though?" asked Sierra. I sat for a moment and pondered that excellent question.

"Linda could have stumbled onto Lena's dirty laundry," I suggested. Sierra remained quiet while she concentrated.

"Did you realize the Commissioner's daughter also has time unaccounted for before she, too, vanished? Her husband, Richard, told police his wife had attended an aerobics class the night before she disappeared. The aerobic instructor told police she came to class, but left abruptly 15 minutes into the session with no explanation and this wasn't the first time she skipped her class.

Yet her husband claimed she returned home that evening at the usual time almost three hours later. Then the following morning when she left the house and took her children to school, she never returned home. There's a pattern here somewhere and we're missing it, Alix. Why hadn't we picked up on this vital piece of information before?" Sierra looked a bit frustrated as I moved around the desk to glance over her shoulder.

"I think we need to go back six months prior to the date of each victim's actual disappearance and examine their daily movements. We might be able to find some type of bond between these women. I have a gut feeling they personally knew each other, Alix." Sierra leaned back in her chair. Unexpectedly, the vibration of my cell phone startled me. I grabbed it immediately. The call came up restricted.

"This is Agent Becker," I answered.

"Alix, can you hear me?" whispered a soft voice.

"Who is this?" I asked with hesitation.

"Alix, you're in danger. Lena never left. Get off the case, Alix! You and your friend need to get off the case before it's too late!" Suddenly, the connection was broken.

"Who was it?" asked Sierra. I stood for a moment in awe. I could have sworn it sounded like Sandy, but I could not be absolutely sure.

"I have a terrible feeling it was Sandy; an unfortunate victim of the condescending hand belonging to Lena," I replied worriedly.

"What did she say?" pressed Sierra.

"She said we were in danger and that we should get off the case and, interestingly enough that Lena never went back to Washington D.C.," I repeated.

"Alix, we need hard core evidence to connect Lena to any one of these victims. Unfortunately, even if Lena did have sex with Linda Haley, it doesn't mean she had her murdered." Sierra went back to searching through the records.

"It's too coincidental…" Sierra didn't bother to finish. I knew exactly what she meant without saying another word.

"Are you thinking what I'm thinking?" I asked. My heart skipped a beat. Sierra's face lit up with excitement.

"What would you think about a women's club perhaps or better yet, a private organization just for women of wealth and stature. What do you think?" A tiny grin formed across her lips.

"There's no law against an elite group of rich and powerful snubbed nose women getting together!" I exclaimed providing Sierra with an open door.

"You know it's more than that especially if several of them are coming up dead!" Sierra was pumped.

"What if, by chance, someone in the organization turned against the others because of jealousy or even perhaps revenge? I think motives are endless when it comes to powerful women." Sierra made a definite point.

"As far as we know, Lena Harris could be a major part of this secret group which would account for her dissociated interest in solving the investigation," continued Sierra. It made total sense and I completely agreed with Sierra's theory.

"A point of contact?" asked Sierra. I thought quietly for a moment.

"Well, where could they conveniently meet without drawing too much attention? Hmmm...I have a wild idea. Let me check real estate properties that have been sold or even rented inside the last three years. I'll base my geographical location within the area where most of the victims had been discovered. If these women met on a regular basis, I'm sure it wasn't at someone's house. No, they would have to gather undetected somewhere secluded and off the beaten path." My mind was racing with interesting thoughts.

"You may be on to something, Alix, and your best bet is to start by using the internet." Sierra seemed pleased with the progress we had finally made.

"I'll go online as soon as I get home tonight." I was busily gathering my things together in order to leave.

"I'll finish the report to the Agent in Charge. You know he'll be on our backs when he gets wind of the fact that I sent confidential material to the President's advisor without his review." Within minutes we were both inside the damp FBI parking lot. We stood in an awkward silence.

"Alix, I just want to say," Sierra blushed slightly, "you're a wonderful woman." With those sweet words lingering in the nippy air, she quickly slipped into her car and left me alone. I smiled to myself while I imagined what it would be like to go home each and every day with this beautiful woman. For the first time in a long time, I felt a true sense of serenity, but more importantly, an unmistakable feeling of inner contentment.

CHAPTER 11

The real estate listings had been a long shot. It was a tedious and time consuming project, but I felt this was a major piece of the puzzle that needed to be solved in order to successfully move ahead with the investigation. It seemed futile after three long hours of continuous research. My eyes burned from staring at the laptop screen. I was just about to give up for the night when something strange caught my eye. I couldn't wait to share my discovery with Sierra.

I took the liberty and arrived early the next morning. Immediately I logged online and found the interesting website. I immediately began running off the information for Sierra to read.

"Anything?" questioned Sierra as she rushed inside my office.

"Here, take a look for yourself; tell me what you think?" I replied. Sierra flipped meticulously through the mounting pages I had stacked neatly on the table.

"Alix, we're searching for specifics. It will take me a week just to look through this wall of paper," Sierra replied exasperated.

"I'm sorry, Sierra. This is the information I would like you to focus on." Instantly, Sierra began to read my highlighted summary.

"This is quite interesting…the old Taylor mansion in South Euclid. It was registered as a historical building back in 1989. It says here that in 1995, after the last of the Taylor descendants passed on, the State took ownership. Then in 1996 an overseas developer purchased the property in its entirety. Plans were to demolish the mansion and put up a mini mall, of all things. At the time, this didn't sit too well with the Mayor of South Euclid so he had an injunction put in place against the demolition company." Sierra remained silent for a moment then continued on.

"Seems the Mayor used his contacts and was able to maneuver the City of South Euclid into a position to buy the property for historical purposes. For years it had been used for school field trips, city picnic gatherings, wedding ceremonies and conferences. Finally, about three years ago, the city placed the property on the market because the renovations became too costly. Three years ago it was sold to a private owner." Sierra stopped reading.

"And the name of this private owner?" I asked quizzically with a huge smile on my face.

"Mr. Harris Lenn?" Sierra looked confused. I couldn't believe she did not see the connection.

"Harris Lenn—Lena Harris?" I felt a bit frustrated by her lack of foresight.

"Don't you see? This is the perfect cover up! Lena decides to take control of the organization and those who defy her methods were murdered! Perhaps their intentions all started in good faith until Lena Harris joined them and then things got out of hand. You even said she didn't need a reason for her immoral and unethical actions. What better place to hold secluded gatherings than an old historic mansion? Its history alone is an excellent cover up for any type of probing questions. And best yet it sits about a half mile off the road. Who's going to put two and two together?" I thought for sure, now that I explained my theory, Sierra would slowly come around to my side.

"You know, Alix, we could be totally wrong with this entire scenario." Sierra immediately decided to become the devil's advocate.

"Sierra, you know we're right. Now we just have to prove it. I say let's take a ride out to the old Taylor place and check it out and see for ourselves." I looked eagerly for her approval and agreement.

"Okay, I'll give you that much, Alix. Make the arrangements and let's see where it takes us," agreed a doubtful Sierra.

Silence filled the car as we drove out to the Taylor mansion. Our unexpected lovemaking on the debriefing room floor had not been brought up nor discussed. I did not want to invade on Sierra's privacy. I felt content holding her soft warm hand as we sat together in the front seat. Her long narrow fingers intertwined lightly with mine. Sierra glanced over at me every now and then with an odd smile across her attractive face. She didn't need to say a word; her beautiful eyes held the truth.

We were scheduled to meet with Heather Walpe, the caretaker of the estate. She agreed to give us a brief tour of the building. The dirt driveway twisted and turned until we finally reached the front entrance. It was majestic in the least. The European style red stone structure presented to be quite impressive. Three enormous towers rose elegantly to the four story walkways which connected each crown. Encompassing each level were several meticulously etched stained glass windows made of the finest cut from beveled European glass. Skirting along the front of the mansion hung noble gables, imported specifically from France, which had been artistically ground and polished.

"Wow," I mumbled under my breath.

Heather had been outside anxiously awaiting our arrival. She was a young woman in her late twenties with dark red hair that bounced playfully about her oval face. But it was her bubbly personality along with her sparkling brown eyes which could have lit up a room. Heather stood tall about 5'8" in flat shoes and her pear shaped body was backed by an overwhelming white pearly and welcoming smile.

"Good day to you ladies! I am Heather Walpe, the caretaker here at the former Taylor's Mansion." Along with the introduction, she eagerly held out her long thin fingers.

"Heather! Thank you for meeting us on such short notice. I'm Linda Duncan and this is Sue Pernel. We are reporters for the *Press.*" Everyone exchanged warm handshakes.

"I understand you are writing an article on buildings built pre-1900. Your superior was quite incisive about a personal tour of the mansion when we spoke." Heather vigorously rubbed her hands together in defiance of the brisk wintery weather.

"Yes. We wanted to bring national awareness to such a valuable treasure like the William Taylor mansion," I gloated gleefully. Sierra threw a sharp glance my way.

"Please, please, let's go inside where it's much warmer." Heather politely held open the huge wooden door.

"You must understand that Mr. Lenn is in the process of restoring and renovating many of the rooms inside the mansion. This spring he plans on bringing in a highly renowned landscaper to emulate that of a Mediterranean countryside in France for the surrounding grounds." We both nodded as Heather continued on with the informative tour.

"We were hoping to meet with Mr. Lenn. Is this possible?" I asked knowing full well of the unlikelihood of such an encounter.

"Mr. Lenn is a very private individual," she replied politely.

"Have *you* ever met Mr. Lenn?" asked Sierra trying to catch her off guard. Heather stopped abruptly and seemed a bit bewildered by the unusual question.

"Why do you ask?" questioned Heather. Small beads of sweat began to form along her hairline.

"Well, we were wondering if you could tell us a little something about the real Mr. Lenn. What type of man he is: adventurous, humorous, boring, etc." I asked immediately taking up where Sierra left off. I hurriedly began scribbling upon my notepad.

"It would add such fullness to the story if we could relate man to mansion," I commented anxiously.

"No, I'm sorry, ladies, I've never met Mr. Lenn, that is, in person. All correspondence is sent to me via email. I have spoken with him many times on the telephone, but he prefers to conduct his business mainly using his computer." Heather purposely turned her face away. She did not lie very well.

"Shall we begin?" stated Heather rhetorically. Sierra and I both nodded with huge smiles plastered across our faces. Heather seemed a tad nervous as we began our journey through the vaulted foyer that led gracefully into an exquisite dining area. Here, an eloquent cathedral ceiling was situated high above, while lavish brocade curtains hung flawlessly on each side of the elongated stained glass windows.

"This is the formal dining area where William Taylor spent many enjoyable evenings eating dinner with his family. As you may already know, he built this house for his ailing wife. She passed away unexpectedly only a few months after completion of the mansion. Mr. Taylor was a busy eccentric but once his Millie had moved on, he vowed to keep close his two children. Since Mr. Taylor's overseas business kept him abroad several months of the year, this truly would become a difficult feat. So he entrusted his children to that of a nanny and the devoted household servants. Shall we move on?" asked Heather. I hurriedly jotted down insignificant notes while she spoke.

"Does Mr. Lenn use this room for dinner meetings?" questioned Sierra. Heather sighed heavily.

"Yes, quite often," replied Heather who seemed a bit irritated by the constant questions regarding the mysterious Mr. Lenn.

"Please, follow me," requested Heather with a half-grin.

As we continued throughout the mansion, it was hard not to be astounded by the amazing beautiful hand carved woodwork which had been lavishly preserved from the period dating all the way back to the year 1838. Antique art pieces were sporadically displayed within heavy glass protective cases. The preservation of this type of historical structure, along with its extreme verse and style of textiles and decorative objects, could only be accomplished by a steady stream of large amounts of flowing cash.

"This is the master suite where William Taylor had slept. As you can see, the bayed sitting area gives way to an endless collection of historical manuscripts dating back well to the beginning of the 1800's." Heather seemed pleased by her extensive knowledge of the Taylor mansion.

"While the tray ceiling lends drama, it is eloquently followed by the imported marble master bath." Heather beamed with knowhow as she hurriedly turned to exit the room.

"Are there any secret corridors hidden within the walls?" I asked. Heather cleared her throat for a second before continuing on with her tour speech.

"The walls were built during a time of unsettlement among the states. Hidden rooms, secret compartments and underground escape routes can be seen on the original set of blue-prints," rattled Heather. Sierra and I quickly glanced at one another. Suddenly, Heather's cell phone chimed.

"Excuse me, I must take this call." We stopped outside the mammoth doors which visibly led into a round study area. By the worried look on Heather's face, I had an unsettled feeling the tour was about to end.

"I am truly sorry, but it seems I must return to my duties. There is a small brochure on the table near the front door which is very informative and may be of use to you when writing your article." Our pace quickened as we were hurriedly ushered out the front door. Heather gave each one of us her business card.

"If I can be of further assistance, please call me. Good day, ladies." Without uttering another word, Heather nervously closed the wide heavy door. The late afternoon air was damp and cool. Sierra and I took our time strolling back to the car. The sodden grounds were covered with a light dusting of fresh snow.

"What do you think?" asked Sierra.

"I think she got spooked by her phone call," I replied.

"Yes, I agree." Sierra backed up and turned the vehicle around.

"Did you notice she didn't say a word while she was on the phone?" I asked.

"Yes. Alix, we need to get back inside and finish the tour on our own." I looked at Sierra then smiled at her late arrival of initiative.

We decided to wait until nightfall before heading back out to the Taylor mansion. We were hoping Heather Walpe had been long gone leaving the old dwelling deserted.

"It looks as if we're alone." I glanced up and scoured the stained glass windows. I instantly pulled my coat tighter as I shivered from the frigid northerly breeze.

"Wait! There's some sort of light illuminating from the second story," whispered Sierra. I squinted straining my burning eyes and tried to focus on the area of concern.

"Maybe the lights are on a timer to dissuade entry by unwanted visitors, like us," I replied sarcastically.

"Sierra, were here, come on," I insisted.

"I don't know about this, Alix. Perhaps this isn't such a good time to be exploring the mansion looking for evidence. After all, what we are about to do is illegal, my dear." Sierra backed up a bit and once again surveyed the darken windows.

"Wait a minute; wasn't this your idea to come back after hours? Okay, you call the shots. What do you want to do, Sierra?" I could feel the blustery wind chill my bones while I waited patiently for Sierra's decision.

"Alright, let's get this over with and get out of here. I still don't like it. Just remember, technically we'll be breaking and entering which doesn't wear too well with the Bureau." Sierra's concerns were noted as we gingerly moved about looking for a way inside the Taylor mansion.

"Let's go around back; perhaps we'll find an unlocked window." We both walked cautiously through the newly fallen snow.

"I see something!" exclaimed Sierra. There, under the moonlit night sky, were two oversized wooden handles.

"It's an old cellar or coal bin. I'm sure this will lead directly into the basement," explained Sierra. As we both pulled and tugged at the resisting bulky doors, the image of Lena Harris suddenly popped into my mind. Within seconds, a tremendous creak then moan emulated as it gradually gave way to the point of entry. The angle was steep. Sierra and I slowly made our descent down the rotting steps into the dark and dingy cellar. The overwhelming smell of mold and mildew hung heavy in the air. The powerful stream of illumination shining from our flashlights exposed the long and stringy cobwebs which clung loosely to the low hanging beams.

"We're fortunate there is no security system," I whispered. Sierra remained silent. The basement was empty except for the remains of broken down crates.

"There's got to be a stairway. Let's look over there." Sierra shined her flashlight across the area.

"Wait a second, did you hear that? It sounds like…" Instinctively, Sierra and I stopped dead in our tracks. Muffled voices could be heard above. Within an instant, a long narrow beam of light floated down just a few feet away. With ease, we silently moved apart and hid along the coarse smelly walls. Neither one of us dared to make a sound nor move from our undetected position.

"Where did she say they were?" asked a deep female voice.

"Somewhere near the far end of the wall," chimed the other woman. Their stream of light wavered back and forth.

"Cobwebs; how I hate spiders!" complained the second woman.

"You're afraid of a little spider, yet you'll snap a man's neck and kill him in an instant without giving it a second thought? Hmmm, what's wrong with that picture?" The other woman chuckled low.

"That's different! Look, let's get what we came for and get back to the meeting. You know how impatient she can be," the woman insisted in a frightened voice. An old door creaked open and the two women gathered dusty bottles from a deteriorated wooden wine rack.

"Be careful!" one of them shouted.

"She'll have our heads if we break even one bottle!" Fear rose in her voice as the sound of scuffling feet hastily exited from the basement.

"Alix, are you okay?" whispered Sierra. I felt her presence nearby.

"That was too close!" I quietly replied.

"Were you able to see their faces?" asked Sierra. By now, Sierra had made her way to my side and slipped her warm hand within mine. Her tepid breath thawed my cold cheeks.

"Not really," I answered.

"Do you remember the Senator from Arizona who was found with his neck broken inside his hotel suite?" questioned Sierra.

"Yes. They never found the killer. In fact they even thought it may have been a…woman!" Sierra pulled back a bit and aimed her flashlight on the ascending steps.

"You think maybe it's a coincidence?" I whispered in doubt.

"I don't know, but I have this horrible feeling these women are up to no good and now we're right in the middle of it." Sierra moved toward the beckoning stairway.

"Let's go find out," she said while gently tugging at my hand. The crumbling staircase shifted from our combined weight. All at once, the weakened steps gave way and we clumsily tumbled to the graveled dirty floor.

"We're not getting too far!" I swore in vain under my breath. Gratefully, neither one of us had been hurt by the slight mishap.

"We'll have to find another way upstairs," commented Sierra. We carefully searched the entire area of the basement. I just about had given up when Sierra spotted our ride.

"Well, well, look what we have here; a dumb waiter." Sierra pulled on the tattering ropes.

"Think it will hold us?" asked Sierra. I ran my hand along the fraying twine.

"No," I replied in all honesty.

"There's one way to find out." Sierra slipped inside. One of the beams snapped.

"Pull me up, Alix." Sierra shut off her flashlight.

"Sierra, you don't even know if this contraption will work and where you'll land!" I whispered hoarsely.

"I'm sure it's the kitchen area. Come on before it breaks into pieces," she persisted. I heaved a heavy sigh. With all my muscle I pulled and yanked. Slowly, but surely, Sierra began to rise into the darkness. When I could pull no more, I tied the splitting vine to the metal hook mounted on the brick basement wall. I waited patiently in the dark. Within seconds Sierra's voice trailed back to me.

"Pull yourself up, we're wasting time." Sierra's words came through mumbled, but I knew exactly what she had wanted me to do. Unfortunately, I knew this would not be an easy task since leverage and strength were the two key elements when using a dumb waiter. And it didn't help the situation that the ropes were frayed and weak. But somehow, with a little luck, and a lot of brute strength, I finally inched my way and reached the top.

The room in its entirety was monstrous in comparison to that of an ordinary household kitchen. An old fashion wood burning stove receded into the oval shaped cement wall. A handsomely designed butcher-block table sat anchored to the floor at the far end of the room. On the counter, a heavy wooden cutting block embellished several large cutting knives while dangling from above swayed a few tarnished pots and pans.

"I think they are meeting in there," mouthed Sierra while pointing to an adjourning room. Suddenly, without any warning, the murmuring voices became unexpectedly clear.

"Quick, follow me!" Sierra snatched my hand and pulled hard. In our desperate attempt to conceal our whereabouts, Sierra seized an uncalculated risk and turned the enormous doorknob. Resounding groans of protest echoed loudly against the aging walls.

"Wait! I don't hear them anymore," I whispered loudly as I leaned in close to Sierra. Her breathing remained calm unlike mine as my heart raced in anticipation of an untimely confrontation.

"You're right, I think they moved on," whispered Sierra. For a moment we relaxed at our small victory of remaining undiscovered.

"What's in here?" asked Sierra. The aged study desperately was in need of a refreshing face lit, but in a strange sense it still retained its original style of elegance and royalty. Directly built into the walls were bookshelves lined from the floor to the ceiling stuffed with antiquated books. The smell of rotting paper and burnt fire wood consumed the air. Massive mounds of gossamer cobwebs hung low from the sagging rafters. The overstuffed Victorian style couches sat unused covered with a thick layer of dust and grime. Old-fashioned reading chairs with high backs and thick armrests sat tattered and torn. Dirty tinted reading lamps rested on tiny round wooden-tables. Thick gaudy drapes covered the only tangible source of light. A soot covered fireplace beckoned to be cleaned.

"Someone had a fire burning in here recently." I scanned the room for any other signs of life.

"Come on, there has to be another way out of here," suggested Sierra. Within seconds, Sierra began to feel the scaly mortar stones surrounding the fireplace.

"What are you doing?" But before Sierra could relate her intentions, the wall shifted exposing a secret passage way.

"How did you know?" I shook my head in disbelief. Sierra smiled then eagerly shined her flashlight into the dark ominous foyer.

"Let me lead the way." Once again, she took my hand, but this time I held on tight. The scent of burning candles filled the dim lit corridor.

"Sierra, how did you know about the secret handle and passage way?" I asked quizzically. She stopped for a second and aimed the beam of light directly under her chin.

"I didn't; I just acted on a hunch. Actually, I saw it before in a movie." Sierra smiled then forged ahead with determination.

The narrow passageway at times became difficult to maneuver and our ambitious walk turned out to be more like a crawl. Layers of dust and dirt hung heavy in the stifled air. The old wooden beams supporting the thick mahogany panels had begun to disintegrate and were in desperate need of renovation.

"I wish I knew where we were at this point? Do you honestly think we'll find a way out?" And before Sierra could answer, she held her finger to her lips.

"Shhhh! I hear music," whispered Sierra. I strained to listen as Sierra took it upon herself to investigate the mysterious tunes.

"Sierra, be careful we don't know how sturdy the walls…" And then it happened! Within a second Sierra disappeared and I stood alone inside the empty corridor.

"Sierra! Sierra!" I called out frantically in a harsh whisper. Suddenly, the strange melody had stopped.

"Seize her!" commanded a loud authoritative voice. I deliriously searched the wall for some kind of way to rescue Sierra. But instead all I found was the amateur carving of two small peepholes. My eyes grew wild in disbelief as the darken forms took on human shapes. Inside the room a bizarre scene of lesbian erotica was taking place on a huge round mahogany table in the center of the room. There, encircling the entwined naked centerpiece, were three rows of masked women seductively dressed in tight black leather attire. Once again, a low hum of chants began to fill the air. I desperately moved about to see the fate of Sierra. It was then I saw a tall shapely masked woman in red. Her long muscular legs accentuated her solid mid section while complimenting her thin waistline. Bright red and skin tight leather straps pulled provocatively across her broad and well developed shoulders. Sierra, bound and gagged, struggled helplessly as her overpowering adversary loomed above.

"Silence!" shouted the evil looking woman. The whole room became quiet at her command. She roughly grabbed and pulled Sierra's hair then leaned in close and whispered something in her ear. Unexpectedly, the woman in red released her hold and kissed Sierra harshly on the lips. As the two husky women held Sierra still, the devilish woman in command violently ripped then tore at Sierra's clothes. It took only seconds for Sierra's unprotected body to become the center of the crazed group of women's sexual obsession. I watched in horror as Sierra resisted with vigor against the endless gloved hands that ravaged her unwilling body. I cursed myself for being weak then closed my tearing eyes at the devastating and horrendous sight. Sierra's continuous cries for help had been silenced from the cloth shoved deep inside her mouth. Then, with one swift punch to Sierra's face, she no longer put up a fight. Once again, the room filled with chants as the deviant leader paced back and forth in front of Sierra's crumpled body. Suddenly, the woman in red raised her hands high in the air and began to speak.

"We have an intruder among us! A traitor within our own flesh and blood! She is not here for the *truth!* We *are* the truth!" proclaimed the wicked leader.

"*We are the truth! We are the truth! We are the truth!*" By now, all the leather bound women were standing and shouting in unison. Sierra, sadly enough, had regained consciousness just in time to see the malice woman sadistically plunge a syringe into her arm. Instantly, Sierra's face filled with fear as the deadly solution of poison surged throughout her veins.

"Where there is one, there is another! Find her!" shouted the beastly leader. It struck me odd she knew of my presence as my mind tried to focus on her threatening words. Of course, I would be of no use to Sierra if I should be apprehended. This deviant woman was playing a dangerous game. My mind darted back and forth trying desperately to think of a safe place to hide or it would be the end for the both of us. With utter desperation, I turned on my flashlight and hurriedly continued down the dark corridor. Beads of sweat dotted my forehead as I searched urgently for a place of refuge.

I was just about to give up when a wild idea struck me. I flashed the light along the side support beams that climbed to the ceiling. With a little luck and a huge miracle, I just might be able to pull it off. I didn't have time to analyze the limited possibilities. I had to take a chance and so with ease and grace, I gingerly scrambled up the sagging beams toward the dark enclosure. I prayed it would hold my weight and conceal my whereabouts.

It wasn't long before the trail of leather covered women closed in and rushed through the corridor below. Shouts of undecipherable words bounced back and forth among the mansion walls. My hands began to ache from the stress of holding my body awry. Sweat dripped carelessly down the sides of my face as I heard the last sounds of the search pass under me. Daringly, I finally relieved my strained body and shimmied back down into the empty passageway. I anxiously expelled a huge sigh a relief when suddenly a familiar voice spoke from within the shadows and shook my victory.

"Alix, if she finds you, she *will* kill you!" Her soft gentle tone burned my ears with fear.

"It's me," the woman whispered. Immediately, I recognized the voice.

"Sandy? Is that you?" I questioned in disbelief. Her unique dress was the same as the others, yet her lovely face remained uncovered free from the concealing mask. I stood awestruck as I gazed into her memorable eyes.

"You've got to leave, Alix. They won't stop until they find you and when they do you will die. It's too late for your friend. I'm sorry, Alix." Sandy tried to explain as anger and resentment depleted my rationale reasoning.

"I'm not leaving without Sierra. So either help me, Sandy, or go on your way," I hissed.

"You don't understand, Alix. These are no ordinary women. They hold powerful and political positions. Do you think they are just going to let you and your friend stroll in and expose their whole operation? Do you? Alix, we're talking about Supreme Court Judges, wives of Senators, even Congresswomen; Mayors and Deans of colleges and universities. The list goes on and on. It all comes down to strength in numbers..." Sandy became quiet.

"Why?" I asked quizzically with venom in my voice.

"How do you move a man-made world, Alix? Behind every great man there is a greater woman. We *are* the truth!" exclaimed Sandy.

"I'm not leaving without Sierra!" I pushed Sandy aside.

"*She* won't let you or Sierra leave here alive. You both know too much, already." Sandy took a step closer then gently touched my arm.

"You must leave, Alix, before it's too late." I instantly pulled away from her touch.

"Who's the leader, the one in red?" I demanded. Sandy looked away and could not face me. I knew in an instant by her troubled expressions.

"Of course, the one and only, Lena Harris." The words tumbled from my mouth.

"Lena will not stop until you are both dead. You have to get out, Alix. Sierra's already dead." My eyes filled with tears at the thought of losing the love it took me so long to find.

"No, she's not! I don't believe you! If you won't help me, I'll find her myself." I urgently moved about and blindly started back.

"Wait! I'll help you, Alix, on one condition," bargained Sandy.

"If I lead you to Sierra, you must promise to leave here and never return."

My legs felt a bit shaky from the news of Sierra's eminent death.

"It's a deal. But how do you know I won't come back with the cavalry?" I asked.

"It doesn't matter. You compromised security and we'll be long gone before you return." Sandy remained serious.

"Sandy, how did you get involved in all of this and how is Lena connected to the murders?" I eagerly pushed for answers.

"I had no choice. She made me a part of this organization despite my objections. As for the murders, yes, each of the victims was a willing member," informed Sandy.

"Why kill them?" I questioned.

"Their dead because they disagreed with Lena's strict and disciplined rules. Once you join with these women, the only possible way of leaving is death. You must realize, Alix, they truly believe that one day women will rule the world! They fantasy about the days when there will be no hierarchy of men—only women." Sandy seemed genuinely frightened by this outlandish way of thinking.

"We must go now before they find us both. I'm pretty sure I know where they took Sierra. She will be heavily guarded, but I have a plan. Let's go!" Our escape through the secret passageway was strenuous. Sandy's familiarity through the hidden corridors turned out to be a life saving asset. It wasn't long before Sandy and I had found Sierra.

"Do not let anyone, I mean anyone, into this room to see this traitor! Is that understood!" yelled Lena Harris. The two hefty leather fitted women nodded to her direct command. Lena exited the room in a rush. Sierra lay unconscious on a small white cot. Thankfully, she appeared to be still alive.

"She doesn't look good," I whispered to Sandy while I peered through the small hole.

"We don't have much time. You wait here!" But before I could protest, Sandy dashed away leaving me alone behind the paneled wall. Within minutes she reappeared inside the room where Sierra had been taken captive.

"You are not allowed to be here! This is a specific order from the commander," spouted the shorter of the two women. Her mask had been removed revealing an attractive face. She looked a bit familiar to me, but I couldn't quite place where I had seen her before. And then it dawned on me. She's was the wife of Senator McGaver from Utah.

"How dare you confront me? Her Excellency wants the prisoner moved!

She'll be dead soon and we need to dispose of the body properly!" Sandy gave a most convincing performance. Hopefully, the two guards would take the bait. The taller of the two eyed Sandy suspiciously.

"Well, what are you waiting for?" Sandy crossed her arms in front of her. The two leathered women looked at one another then proceeded to do as they were told. As they both leaned over to lift Sierra, Sandy quickly plunged a syringe full of sedation in each one of their backs.

"Aaaagghh!" cried the Senator's wife before she fell unconscious to the floor. The other woman, who was much larger, was a bit more resistant. With minimal force, Sandy slung a hard fist straight into her face causing her to recoil and drop next to her fallen comrade. Sandy then dragged both women into the large walk in closet and then locked them inside. Urgently, she felt for a pulse on Sierra's limp arm.

"She's alive, Alix!" shouted Sandy. My heart raced faster and I was more than eager to get Sierra and leave this place.

"We have to stay quiet so no one hears us. I know another way out behind the walls. With any luck we'll be long gone before Lena learns of our escape!" Sandy pulled at the candle light fixture that hung above the small fireplace in the bedroom. Instantly, the paneled piece in front of me opened liked a door. It didn't take me long before I held Sierra sadly in my arms. Tears slipped down my flushed cheeks.

"There's no time for this, Alix, we need to get her to a hospital before it's too late," insisted Sandy.

"Let me help you with her." So between the two of us we were able to semi-lift then carry Sierra through the small opening. But once inside it became extremely difficult to maneuver her weaken state within the cramp and narrow passageway.

"Sandy, I can't have you risk your life for us. Go before Lena discovers it was you who betrayed her. I'll figure something out." Sandy slowly released Sierra's arms.

"She'll kill the both of you, Alix. I'll try to distract Lena long enough for you to remove Sierra from danger." With that she kissed me quickly on the cheek and disappeared into the darkness.

I urgently began to drag Sierra's body along the filthy dusty floor. Every now and then I could hear mumbled voices from behind the walls. My back began to ache and my arms felt pulled as I tugged at her flaccid body. At this pace, it would take me all night before reaching the library where Sierra and I had first started. There had to be a better way. But as I stopped briefly to relieve my sore muscles, I heard the cry of wolf.

"Commander, the prisoner is missing!" shouted a deep voiced woman.

"Find them and bring them to me!" ordered Lena. The shuffle of feet could be heard as they scurried away to search for Sierra and me. I gently laid Sierra's body down to try and look through the cracks. There stood Lena and Sandy face-to-face and alone.

"Where are they?" hissed Lena. Lena's hand lingered along Sandy's breasts.

"You enjoy my touch, don't you?" Sandy closed her eyes and did not respond. Lena then began to caress the tender spot between Sandy's slim thighs.

"I can give you pleasure like no other," whispered Lena as she sensually licked Sandy's cheek. A slight moan escaped through Sandy's lips. Then suddenly, without warning, Lena roughly grabbed Sandy's hair and pulled back hard.

"You're hurting me, Lena!" cried Sandy. Lena's other hand quickly wrapped around Sandy's throat.

"Do you honestly believe you can outsmart me?" Lena's words dripped with hate.

"No one is smarter than you, Lena." Sandy could barely choke out an answer. Her face was beginning to turn blue from lack of oxygen. I stood watching helplessly knowing I couldn't do a thing to help save Sandy from Lena's lethal hold.

"I could snap your neck like a twig if I chose to do so!" Lena lessened her death grip then unsparingly shoved Sandy to the floor.

"Why do you protect them?" demanded Lena with venom. Sandy tried desperately to catch her breath.

"Let them go, Lena. They don't know anything. In fact, they don't even know who you are!" pleaded Sandy.

"No, they are traitors to the cause. They do not seek the truth. They'd rather live in a chaotic world filled with dominating men who treat women as slaves." Lena nervously paced back and forth across the room.

"Sandy, I thought you were one of us. I thought you believed in our fight for truth. But most of all...I thought you believed in me!" Lena was down on the floor next to Sandy. Sandy instinctively threw her arms around Lena's neck and held her close. After a second or two, the embrace had ended.

"Come and help me find the intruders." Lena stood up with an outstretched gloved hand. Sandy's eyes filled with tears.

"I will follow my commander," chanted Sandy.

My attention turned to Sierra who still laid unconsciousness. I began to panic at the thought of Sandy turning against us and willing her alliance to such a crazy woman. With all the strength I could muster, I once again tackled the task of dragging Sierra's body to safety. As we turned a bend in the wall, I realized, much to my surprise, the corridor had widened making it easier to transport Sierra. I was almost positively sure this is where we had begun. Then, when I thought Sierra and I were finally in the clear, the unsettled world around us discouragingly collapsed. As we exited into the study through a hidden door, we were greeted by Lena Harris and her band of women in leather.

"Well, well, well, nice of you to drop in again, Alix. Oh, and I see you brought your girlfriend too!" Sarcasm dripped from vile lips of Lena Harris.

"Seize her!" shouted Lena. Several leather fitted women came rushing to my side. I couldn't break their binding hold.

"And you!" Lena Harris pointed her shaky hand straight at Sandy.

"You will suffer the consequences of betrayal! Go and take her to my private chambers! I will deal with her later," commanded Lena.

"Lena, how could you do this to me? I believed in you!" cried Sandy as the two guards savagely roughed her up.

"You made your choice, Sandy. Take her away," mumbled Lena. Sandy fought in desperation as the two overpowering women yanked then dragged her kicking and screaming out the library door. Slowly, Lena turned to face me.

"Give it up, Lena! It's all over! We know about your sadistic cult of women! You'll never get away with any of this!" I struggled to break free but to no avail.

"You fool! Neither one of you will live to tell a single soul. You'll watch your sweetheart die. And then it's your turn!" Lena suddenly smacked me swift and hard across my face. My bottom lip split open wide. A bright red liquid spurted from my wound. For a brief second, my vision blurred, but I fought diligently to try and keep my senses.

"Take them away to the master ceremonial room! Then call all our members so that each may take a turn and leave their mark of truth!" Lena turned abruptly away and left the room. My mind was foggy from the sudden impact. Dizziness and nausea swept over me.

"Move it!" screeched a burly shaped woman as she shoved and pushed me forward. She held a small pistol against the base of my skull as I staggered ahead in pain and confusion.

The ceremonial chamber was dark and dreary. The only visible light was the burning of several torches mounted strategically about the room giving off a mid-evil illusion and aura. The floor was filthy with dirt and grime. Sierra's unconscious body had been dragged and tossed upon what looked to be a sacrificial table. Her body lay limp as they spread her across the cold slab of stone. My heart beat loudly inside my ears as fear swelled up inside. The leather strips which bound my wrists pinched and burned my skin as I urgently struggled for freedom.

"Sisters, are you here for the truth?" Lena cried out.

"We are all here, my lady!" exclaimed a loud voice from the back of the room. Several rows of masked women in tight black leather apparel filled the room. Lena turned and paced a bit near Sierra. She ran her gloved hand down the front of Sierra's unconscious and bruised body. Suddenly, Lena halted and made her way to me.

"Do you my sister want to know the truth?" she hissed through gritted teeth.

"The truth is you're nothing but an insane murderer!" I shouted. I tried so desperately to keep my emotions under control, but the sight of Sierra's lifeless body made my blood boil with overwhelming anger. Without hesitation, Lena once again, slapped my already bloodied face.

"Silence!" Lena then backed away.

"You're a fool, Alix! You could have been one of us! We have the power, the status, the will and the opportunity to be the salvation for all of womankind. Unbelievers, like you and you're sweet ass girlfriend, are obstacles. You're both useless and expendable! You block the way to freedom for all women! You must be punished! *We are the truth*!" Lena's deep threatening voice echoed throughout the enormous room.

"*We are the truth! We are the truth! We are the truth!*" A thunder roll of unison voices shook the ceremonial chamber. The entire group of women raised a fisted hand high up into the air. As the chanting eased into silence, I could feel my binding strips of leather begin to slag. I eagerly relaxed my sore and aching wrists which provided enough slippage to loosen the knot. I desperately needed to buy myself some time.

"What do you hope to accomplish by filling these women with unattainable dreams of grandeur?" My words were slightly slurred as my bottom lip began to swell.

"What did you say about unattainable dreams?" Lena burst into a hideous laughter. The entire room remained silent as Lena spoke.

"These are not mere dreams, but the future of womankind. *We are everywhere!* We are the backbone of this country for without women there is no government. Without women, there is no democracy. Without women, there is no rationale underlying the foundation to this entire country! It is *women* who control the absolute existence of the human race! For without women, there would be no race at all." Lena continued to preach as I meticulously tried to free myself without detection.

"Enough of this!" shouted Lena with anger. My husky sentinel had lowered her weapon long ago and had joined in with the rest of the chanting group. Fortunately, my back faced away unseen by the many eyes, including those of Lena Harris.

"So your big plan is to take over the country and then the world?" I asked sarcastically knowing full well she would silence me again. Within a split second, my assumption had been reaffirmed, but this time a nasty blow to my stomach left me gasping for air then collapsing to the floor.

"Neither you nor your girlfriend will reap the benefits which we shall bestow!" But as I doubled over onto the floor, I swiftly became free of my restraints. Surprisingly, my moves were smooth and precise. I seized this flash of unexpected opportunity and instinctively withdrew the spear pointed serrated knife I had hidden safe inside my Tanker boot.

Even Lena, with all her bouts and cries of ultimate wisdom, could not foresee nor comprehend the magnitude of my irrevocable revenge. And so with full force, I leapt up and plunged the sharp tool deep within the soft flesh under her chin. Instantly, Lena's maddening eyes flew open wide in shock and then disbelief. I gave Lena no chance to retaliate as I thrust the knife even further ripping mercilessly into her brain. Within seconds, streams of bright red blood came pouring from her orifices and the gaping hole I had relentlessly left behind. Lena instinctively cupped her gloved hands around her bleeding neck. In hopeless desperation, she frantically tried to salvage her life that was spilling out onto the floor. As Lena dropped heavily to her knees, her garbled screams became faded. It was all over within one torturing minute. Seconds later, Lena

Harris, lay dead drowned within her own pitiless blood; a crumpled heap of pure evil.

At the astounding revelation that their glorious leader had lost her fight to live, panic seized the entire room and the leather bound women scattered leaving me alone with Lena's listless corpse. It was then I realized my hand was covered with Lena's blood. I stood for a brief moment to soak in the aftershock from my deliverance of justice. It didn't take me long to pull myself together and focus primarily on Sierra. She remained unconscious and unaware of the horrendous trauma that had just transpired before her closed eyes. I gingerly removed Sierra's comatose body from the table and held her close as I hurriedly made the call for an ambulance.

In the meantime, the Taylor mansion had become deserted and wiped clean of any evidence that could possibly divulge the many deep dark secrets hidden and protected within the solidarity of the walls. Sierra had been urgently flown away to an unknown and secluded destination while I, on the other hand, had been unjustly arrested and taken into custody, for the murder of Lena Harris, once a prestige member, on the White House staff.

CHAPTER 12

The four-by-six holding cell was frigid. I shivered, not only from the extreme temperature inside the cell, but from mental and physical exhaustion. The debriefing had been quick and to the point. A specifically hand-picked panel of my so called peers agreed unanimously. Despite my protest of innocence, criminal charges were set forth against me. It was crucial that someone step-up and become the sacrificial offering for this outrageous blunder. And that someone, they decided, would have to be me.

With no set bail or support from the Bureau, I contacted my long time friend and attorney at law, Maria Shiner. Maria and I had been close friends for the past ten years. Her demur was very impressionable in that of a sweet and lovely woman *outside* the courtroom. But inside the halls of justice, she could be ruthless and cunning when the circumstances arose. Maria gladly took on my case and was more than willing to represent me, in my time of need.

Maria was waiting patiently as I was escorted into the room. The cuffs entwined about my wrists had been removed for our brief meeting. Her pearly white smile was refreshing and most welcomed.

"Alix, how are you holding up?" asked Maria from across the battered wooden table. I leaned forward to absorb her warmth and friendship.

"Okay, I guess. It's..." my words trailed off into an unsettled silence. Suddenly, my emotions turned inside. Tears of resentment swelled within brimming beyond my control. For a brief moment, I felt totally alone.

"Alix, I've pulled in a few favors and I'm waiting to hear back about the possibility of bail. It's been difficult considering the extremity of the charges brought against you." I felt a bit relieved by Maria's comforting and familiar face.

"I've studied list of indictments." Maria stopped and looked gently into my tired eyes.

"You have been accused of overstepping your authority by entering a premise without cause or warrant; endangerment of a fellow agent; the intent to kill and what really put the icing on the cake is murder in the first degree." Maria clasped her hands on top of the small stack of papers. For some odd reason, I felt quite embarrassed and dropped my head to stare at the table.

"I believe you are innocent, Alix. I truly believe you had justification for killing Lena Harris. You feared for your life and that of your fellow agent, Sierra Montgomery." But before Maria could continue on, I rudely cut her words in half.

"Where is Sierra? Is she…is she still alive?" Once again, small drops of tears carelessly slipped down my worried face. Maria patted my shaky hands.

"I'm trying to find out where they took her as we speak. It's not an easy task. They put a tight lid on your girlfriend. I think they're afraid she may wake up and collaborate with your testimony which will blow their case right out of the water! Right now, though, we need to get you out of here. Then we can begin to focus on your defense." Maria stood up to leave.

"The next time I come back, I promise you'll be leaving with me." Maria gathered her papers then motioned for the guard outside the door.

"Hang in there and I'll see you soon." The guard issued Maria out while the woman correctional officer, once again, cuffed my sore aching wrists.

"You think you're all that, eh? Once a big time FBI agent, now you're just like the rest of the losers." She flashed a devious grin as she chuckled then roughly pushed and shoved me back to my lonely cell.

Maria came through with her promise. Bail was set for an astronomical tune of $1,000,000. I had no choice, but to deal with a bail bondsmen. After an hour or so of bickering, I reluctantly handed over the deed to my house, the title to my car, and a signed promise not to skip town before my trial date.

I met with Maria several times and worked diligently on defense strategies. Her concerns were genuine, but I still clung to the feeling it would eventually come down to the basic argument of the essential need to survive. The whereabouts of Sierra remained a mystery. Maria had made connections and was cunningly cashing in on some of her aces.

"Maria, I really do appreciate the fact you agreed to take my case. I know that the prosecution might bring up the fact that we are friends and it could be considered a conflict of interest." Maria nodded in agreement.

"Alix, your friendship means more to me than I can put into words. You were there for me when there was no one else. You put yourself out on the line not only personally, but also financially. Your support and confidence gave me the courage I needed to succeed." Maria's eyes glistened under the fluorescent lights.

"That's what friends are for," I whispered.

"I'll be completely honest with you, though, when you told me about your predicament, I literally jumped at the chance to defend you. I knew if anyone could help you, it would be me." Maria's voice was full of emotion.

"It's been a long time since you started your practice from home. I remember the day so clearly when we first met. You were this young, naïve upcoming lesbian attorney who was struggling for a place in the justice system. I, on the other hand, was not too sure of myself either while I testified, as an expert witness, in court." We both chuckled at our memories. Then suddenly her smile instantly vanished from her lovely face. Maria abruptly turned away with her back facing me.

"I don't know how to say this, but I was ordered to make sure you never walked the streets again, especially as a Federal Agent." I could barely hear Maria's voice. But the ramifications of what I thought I just heard had stripped away any form of a fair trial. I knew instantly Maria had been warned by certain political advisors at the White House.

"Maria, I understand completely…" But Maria did not let me finish.

"And…I told these particular individuals that I was your attorney and would defend you as such. They were not happy in the least." Maria quickly turned around then nervously paced back and forth.

"I guess I don't need to ask who is doing the squeezing," I commented.

"I couldn't tell you if I wanted to, Alix. You're better off not knowing. These…these gold diggers are powerful people. They are looking for blood— your blood, Alix, to be spilled all over the courtroom. They have the means to make you disappear and to make my life a living hell, especially since I basically told them to shove it. It won't be long before I feel the downswing of their wrath." Maria slowly shook her head.

"Alix, over the years as a defense attorney, I have done some things…well, that doesn't matter right now, but as *your* attorney and most of all, your friend, I promise to provide you with the best possible defense I can give." Maria's smile was weak.

"Thank you, Maria." Maria briefly gave me an encouraging hug before I left her office. The smell of her perfume lingered upon my light colored coat. As the cold night air stung teasingly at my face, my solemn thoughts, once again, turned to Sierra. Each and every day, not knowing whether she was alive or dead, kept me bound to a never ending living hell.

The following day I arrived early for my preliminary hearing. Maria was sitting at a long mahogany table. The bailiff escorted me to a seat right beside Maria.

"I hear the judge is Mary Ellen Cesseran. She's really into women's rights. I feel she will be fair with your case, Alix." Maria was busily scribbling on her notepad.

"Alix, I do have a bit of good news for you; I found Sierra." Instantly, my heart skipped a beat and hope filled my senses.

"I was told she's definitely alive, but still in a comatose state. Her drug induced coma has not been responding to medication. Hopefully, in time her system will right itself and she will heal. I'm sorry, Alix. I wish I had better news for you." Maria lightly squeezed my sweaty hand. By now, the prosecution had taken their place inside the courtroom.

"I have to see her, Maria. Where is she?" I whispered forcefully. But before Maria could answer, the bailiff began his announcement.

"All rise," he bellowed.

"The Honorable Judge Cesseran resides in this courtroom." Judge Mary Ellen Cesseran entered the courtroom through a side wooden door. The heavy set woman was no taller than I. Her relatively attractive face was the only part of her body exposed as the long black silky cape covered her entire extremity. She glided in with extreme confidence and a touch of royalty, then rested comfortably in the tall back cushioned chair. As the entire courtroom returned to their seats, the bailiff loudly read the case number.

"Counselor, how does your client plead to the charges brought against her by the State of Ohio?" asked Judge Cesseran. Maria and I were standing.

"Not guilty, your Honor." Maria's voice was firm and professional.

"Trial date is set four weeks from today. Counselor, does your client understand the necessity of staying within the city limits until the trial date?" Judge Cesseran eyed me with unspoken criticism.

"Yes, she does, your Honor." Maria spoke with fervor. We remained standing long enough for Judge Cesseran to exit the courtroom. Within the hour we were back at Maria's office.

"Alix, is there anyone other than Sierra, who could vouch for what happened at the old Taylor mansion?" questioned Maria. Sandy's name jumped to mind.

"Sandy Lewis. She's a barmaid at the Peastone and a very close friend of Lena Harris. In fact, she was the one who warned me about Lena from the very beginning. When Sierra and I were trapped, Sandy was the one who risked her life to help us escape. Unfortunately, after Sierra and I were captured, they took Sandy and I don't know what happened to her. I was so worried about Sierra; I never bothered to search for Sandy. Then the police arrived and arrested me." Maria remained quiet and still. I knew she was holding back.

"What is it, Maria? What do you know that you're not telling me?" My heart sped up a bit at the thought of Sandy's unfortunate fate.

"The police discovered a blond haired woman with her throat slit in one of the backrooms. They were able to make a positive identification and sadly to say she turned out to be your link, Sandy Lewis." Without reservation, I dropped heavily onto the cushioned chair. My eyes brimmed with burning tears. This poor dear woman had come to meet her untimely death by the sadistic hand which she feared the most. Sandy Lewis had died because she tried to save our lives.

"You do realize that Sierra is the only witness who can testify on your behalf, don't you?" Maria put her arm around my sagging shoulders.

"There's no one else," I whispered while wiping away the drops of grief from my flushed cheeks. Maria sighed deeply.

"Alix, I know this doesn't look good for you, but I promise to do my best." Maria tried to sugar coat the inevitable. In the back of my mind, I knew exactly what this meant; the White House had already passed judgment without even a trial.

CHAPTER 13

Maria's connection came through and she made good on her promise. The drive into the country was pleasant, especially with the creeping rise of the sun in the distant horizon. The wintry mix of low-lying clouds tumbled across the skyline relentlessly as streaming rays of sunshine peaked in and out. I arrived at the sanitarium within two hours. After I checked in at the front desk, I was instructed to meet with the director of the recluse institution.

"Agent Becker, it's a pleasure to make your acquaintance. We've been expecting you." Christa Grodisic held out a strong hand. She stood tall and thin behind the messy metal desk. Her attractive face, surrounded by bouncy brown curls, melted into her lovely smooth skin. The plaid suit she wore fit snug about her round shaped hips. Her deep blue silky blouse hung loose against her well endowed chest.

"Thank you, Ms. Grodisic, for taking the time to see me," I responded courteously.

"It's quite alright, Agent Becker. Please, call me Christa. Formality sometimes just clouds the issue at hand." Her smile was genuine and most refreshing.

"In turn, my name is Alix," I insisted. She nodded in agreement.

"You do realize your friend is still comatose," stated Christa.

"Yes, I know," I replied hesitantly.

"Follow me, then." Christa moved with grace and style.

"We have tried numerous treatments on Ms. Montgomery. You must understand, Agent Becker, I mean Alix, depending on the extent of brain damage; she may never come out of this vegetated state. She could remain just like she is right now for years. And until Ms. Montgomery becomes awake, it is almost impossible to determine the exact parts of the brain that have been traumatized, if that be the case," reported Christa. By now my heart dropped heavily into my stomach. Sierra's prognosis was indeed disheartening, to say the least.

Christa opened yet another set of doors that led down a carpeted hallway. It wasn't long before we arrived at a set of unmarked elevators. Christa inserted a key and the doors opened wide. The elevator inside smelled of grease and oil. Immediately, my investigative instincts kicked back in.

"Has this elevator been serviced lately?" My mind began to race with all sorts of wild speculations. Paranoia had taken control.

"Why, yes? How did you know?" Christa responded quizzically.

"What floor?" I demanded in a huff. Christa was taken back by my sudden rudeness.

"Sierra's room is located on the 5th floor." I urgently pushed at the number five repeatedly hoping it would speed the elevator's ascend. As the doors sprung open, I literally pushed Christa out from within the elevator.

"What room?" I shouted.

"It is the fourth room on the left; but its secure, you need a key…!" Christa tried to explain as I roughly shoved her aside. Within seconds, I hurriedly dashed down the hallway in front of Sierra's room. The door was slightly ajar. Alarms went off inside my head as I quickly retrieved my own personal piece of security that I kept strapped around my calf. By now, Christa had finally joined me.

"What's the meaning of this? We do not allow firearms of any sort…why, this room is supposed to be locked and secured at all times!" exclaimed Christa.

"Get back!" I insisted in a harsh whisper. Immediately, Christa flattened herself against the wall.

The room had been semi-dark with only the glow from the hospital equipment illuminating the several hanging bottles filled with fluids. A slight hum emanated from one of the life support machines. Sierra lay flat on the bed, covered with a white sheet, unaware of me or anything else for that matter. Instinctively, I could sense there was something horribly wrong. Then suddenly, without any warning, the heart monitor blasted a high alert alarm.

"Code Blue! Code Blue!" Christa Grodisic burst in right past me as she radioed for immediate assistance.

"What is it?" I shouted while cautiously making my way to Sierra's bedside.

"She's in cardiac arrest! Stand back!" This time Christa pushed me aside and nervously searched for Sierra's pulse.

"I'm going to jolt her!" Within moments, Christa flipped a switch and grabbed the two oval shaped paddles. I, on the other hand, was focused on the slight movement within her chest.

"Stand back!" yelled Christa as she began to lower the cylinders.

No!" I cried and with brute force I knocked the paddles free from her grip.

"What in heaven's name are you doing? I'm trying to save this woman's life!" screamed Christa as she once again snagged the paddles from off the floor.

"She's breathing! She's breathing!" I shouted. The alarm was still blaring while loud footsteps drew near from the hallway outside.

"That's impossible!" Christa leaned in close to Sierra's face. A small trail of warm air lightly bounced against Christa's cheek. Indeed, Sierra displayed definite signs of life. Once again, Christa searched for a pulse, but this time she found it.

"My heavens, I could have sworn…" Christa, realizing the devastation that could have transpired by her obvious misjudgment, became overwhelmed with dissolution and embarrassment. By now, the room was full of concerned nursing staff.

"This woman…I don't understand. The alarm would have never gone off if she wasn't in a state of cardiac arrest." Christa was noticeably shaken by this whole frightening incident. Sierra lay motionless as her chest slowly moved up and down in time with her slow paced breathing.

"If you didn't stop me, I would have killed her," she whispered as her sorrowful eyes filled with tears. The nursing team was busily checking vital signs and adjusting fluid intake. Christa voluntarily backed away from the bed.

"Someone deliberately tampered with the heart monitor to make it look like she was having a heart attack. I believe someone wanted you to try and save Sierra. They were counting on you, Christa, to do your job and theirs!" I tried to console Christa. Despite all the commotion and near death experience, Sierra remained motionless.

"Christa, we need to check out the person who serviced the elevator. Someone wanted Sierra dead." I walked back over to the heart monitor. Feeling the back of the elongated metal box, I knew immediately someone had been tampering with the switch. Surely they must have known eventually the truth would be found, but by then it would have been too late. Sierra would have died by one fatal act of misjudgment.

It didn't take Christa long before she contacted the elevator company. The manager on duty said a call was never received nor logged from Cranbrook for any type of elevator repair service. He also went on to stress that he was the only person authorized to dispatch a maintenance person out to any privately owned institutions.

"Maintenance workers are thoroughly checked then screened before they are allowed to enter Cranbrook. After they are issued a clearance pass, they are escorted at all times throughout the building. I will get to the bottom of this immediately, Alix." Christa's composure had returned and she was more than determined to find the culprit. She asked me to wait while she talked with the guard at the front gate. It didn't take long before she had a young Hispanic security officer sulking in her office.

"So you're saying, Mr. Gerard, that you left the maintenance worker alone so you could go downstairs to the vending machines for a cup of coffee? What were you thinking? You know the procedures! How long were you gone for heaven's sake?" Christa badgered her victim.

"I don't remember. It couldn't have been that long! Maybe ten minutes at the most. She was still working on the elevator when I got back!" The distressed guard shifted back and forth as he desperately tried to defend his unprofessional behavior. Christa was not so forgiving.

"Wait a second! The maintenance person was a woman?" I knew instantly someone from within the satanic group had been sent to finish the job that Lena had failed to complete. It would have been a precautionary measure to ensure that Sierra never regained consciousness to testify in court.

"Yeah, it was a woman, alright. Good looking, too. Her hair was pulled up under a baseball cap." His eyes lit up as he spoke.

"Did she carry anything with her?" I asked.

"Yeah, an old black leather bag and I checked it out myself. It just had a bunch of tools and a container of elevator grease.

"She used the tools she brought in the bag to tamper with Sierra's life support system. It would be almost impossible to try and track her down, now," I said with disappointment. Christa finished her intense questioning and then suspended the blundering security guard.

"I would still like to visit with Sierra alone, if that is possible," I requested. Christa apologized once again for the mishap and escorted me to Sierra's room.

"I'm sure you can find your way back down when you are finished. I will see you out then; please take your time, Alix." Christa threw me a sympathetic smile as she walked quietly out of the room.

I hesitated a moment before I ever so gently ran my finger down the soft skin of Sierra's discolored arm. She looked so calm and peaceful as she lay there unaware of my existence. I calmly took her hand and held it to my wet face. How could this possibly be happening to Sierra? How could this be happening to me? In a couple of weeks, I would be fighting for my own life as Sierra lays here and fights to keep hers; both of us isolated in our desperate attempt to survive.

"I love you, Sierra. Please, please, come back to me, sweetheart!" The heart monitor beeped while jagged lines appeared on the flat screen. Her lifeless body remained perfectly still. Even though I was finally reunited with Sierra in body, I tried desperately to fight this overwhelming feeling of loneliness in spirit. After about an hour of intense silence, I could handle it no more and reluctantly left Sierra behind.

Christa Grodosic graciously extended her welcome by inviting me back whenever I felt the need to visit Sierra. With the trial only a few weeks away, my visits would be few. Maria had already made prior arrangements with Christa, that if there should be the slightest change in Sierra's condition, communication should be directed immediately to Maria's office. I was grateful for Maria's intuitive hindsight.

"It's about time! What's going on there?" questioned Maria. I could see Maria now pacing back and forth across the room anxiously awaiting my call. I delved right in, non-stop, about the unbelievable episode of Sierra's attempted murder.

"I'm glad Sierra is safe, Alix. The attempt made on Sierra's life could help your case. Let's face it, someone wants Sierra dead. They're afraid she will come out of her coma to testify on your behalf. That adds fuel to the fire. I'm going to make a few phone calls and see if we can't track down the woman who disguised herself as an elevator repair person. I'll arrange to have a guard outside Sierra's room from now on at all times," state Maria.

"I have an idea, Alix. It's a long shot, but what if you were to go back to San Panzel and have another conversation with Mr. James Rascliffe to see if perhaps he possibly had a change of heart," suggested Maria. I agreed with Maria on one thought, it was indeed, a long shot.

"I'm no longer an agent, will that be a problem?" I asked.

"Not unless you want it to be!" exclaimed Maria under a boisterous chuckle. Maria was more than determined to win my case.

CHAPTER 14

Dark clouds hung heavy in the damp cold air as I traveled, this time, alone to San Panzel. Puddles of frozen water lay undisturbed throughout the deserted parking area of the prison. Maria had prearranged an unviewed holding cell for my interrogation with Rascliffe. She needed more information and I intended to get it; one way or another.

The rattling of chains bounced off the sound proof walls. There were only two chairs which sat face-to-face in the middle of the frigid room. I stood as the guards led James inside.

"Sit down, asshole, and don't try anything stupid or I'll bash in your stinking head." The muscle bound correctional officer shoved him roughly onto the seat almost tipping it over. Rascliffe swore, under his breath, at the guard as he left the room. The bolt latched into place from the outside. Rascliffe's left eye was swollen shut. His protruding lower lip revealed a wide red gash. Dried blood still stuck to his cheek.

"What the hell you lookin' at?" he said with a slight lisp. With that unwarranted tone, I stomped heavily on the top of his foot with my steel-tipped boot. His scream echoed within the four concrete walls.

"Ahhh! You dumb…" Rascliffe cried as I cut him off in midstream.

"Naughty, naughty, Mr. Rascliffe! If I didn't know any better, I would be inclined to believe that you could be so stupid to try and call me a vile name!" He hung his head down as he mumbled hateful obscenities.

"Now, you listen, you low life! I need information and if you're not willing to cooperate with me, then I guess maybe I'll just have to beat it out of you. Or better yet, I'll ask your friend, the guard outside, to help me. I bet I can make his day!" And before Rascliffe could respond from his distorted bloody mouth, I quickly moved behind and held him in a deadlock grip. I had to restrain myself from administering just the right amount of pressure, or I could snap his thick neck in half.

"Do you understand?" I whispered harshly in his ear. Rascliffe gasped for air as he pounded frantically at my locked arms. I interpreted this to be a sign of acknowledgment and released my hold. Rascliffe's cuffed hands encircled his sore throat. He coughed and sputtered undecipherable words. Rage consumed his face as spit flung from his grotesque shaped mouth.

"I'm gonna kill you, like I did the rest! I'm gonna cut you up into pieces and scatter your sorry ass all over the place!" shouted Rascliffe. Instinctively, I retracted my Berretta that was strapped to the inside of my boot. I held the cold barrel of steel flush up against his sweaty forehead.

"Go ahead, Rascliffe! Give me the excuse I need to blow your ugly face clear off this planet!" I gripped the gun with two hands then released the safety switch. Rascliffe knew now, I was downright serious. His breathing became labored and perspiration dripped from his forehead down into his narrow beady eyes.

"Now that you understand me, why don't we talk like two rationale human beings? What do you say, Rascliffe?" His eyes never left the barrel of my gun. As his breathing returned to normal, I carefully returned my gun to its proper holder.

"Look, I told you everything the last time you were here." Bloody snot leaked from his right nostril.

"That's not enough," is all I said. Rascliffe's face was distorted with various colors from the fresh injuries he retained from his latest beating from the prison guards.

"I done told you, I don't know anything'!" He spat a huge bloody mass onto the floor. Without warning, I abruptly stood up and grabbed his hair jerking his head back.

"That's not the correct answer, Jimmy Boy! Maybe you need a bit of persuasion…" I threatened as I tapped the side of my leg.

"Alright!" he muffled.

"It was a woman!" James cried as he winced in pain.

"We had already established this fact during our previous conversation," I replied.

"Wait! She'd give me the name and address of the bitch she wanted me to do. She said I could kill her the way I want, but it had to be the same each time." Rascliffe looked down at the floor.

"Since you're such an intelligent gent, I bet you figured out there would be more than just one, eh?" I rocked back in my chair.

"It doesn't take a rocket scientist…never mind!" he mumbled between his two front teeth that had been broken off.

"Did she tell you to rape the women, too?" I asked disgusted by this vile human being. Rascliffe did not answer. I kicked his foot hard.

"No, that was my idea; but I didn't rape them all!" he acknowledged gleefully. A sadist half-grin crossed his battered swollen face.

"So, the same woman gave you the instructions each time, correct?" I questioned.

"Yep, it sounded like the same voice each time. Hell, she even told me I didn't have to worry about being caught that she'd handle all the details." Rascliffe shook his head back and forth with disappointment.

"I should have known I'd catch the wrap," he grumbled.

"How did she know you went through with it?" I further pressed.

"I called her back when I was finished with the job. Then she wired the money to my account," replied James.

"What phone did you use to call her back?" I asked with curiosity.

"The same phone she called me on, the pay phone," he answered. Rascliffe began to fidget in his seat.

"I want to go back to my cell, now. I'm tired of answering your stupid questions," retorted Jimmy Boy.

Rascliffe proceeded to spit a huge wad of crimson snot onto the floor near my boot. Repelled by his vulgar behavior, I made a drastic mistake and moved my chair slightly back. And it was within that brief instant of breaking eye contact with the hired killer Rascliffe seized the minute opportunity and unexpectedly rushed me. But before I could stop his surprise attack, Rascliffe's cuffed hands were tight around my neck choking the life from me. His eyes were dilated with rage. A thick line of spittle dripped onto my cheek. I desperately tried to clear my head as the last bit of oxygen was being forced from my constricted lungs.

Suddenly, Sierra's face flashed before my eyes. Rascliffe thought he had won as my struggle to stay alive dwindled and I began to lose the fight. But just as he was about to claim victory from what he thought to be such an easy battle, my FBI training skills swung in with full force. Instinctively, I gathered together the enormous strength in my legs and encircle his upper torso to break his deadly hold. In one swift move, I pulled him off onto the cold cement floor. This gave me the edge I needed to right myself in the position to heave down with my foot and crush his unprotected neck. Rascliffe was astounded and disappointed that I was not dead. He eagerly tried to suck in air while he feverishly pounded against my stationed leg. Finally, Rascliffe's useless thrashing stopped and his head dropped leadenly to the side. I pulled my boot away from the killer's bruised neck just as the holding cell door opened wide. The hefty guard held a club in one hand and his revolver in the other.

"You okay, Agent Becker?" he asked with genuine concern.

"Fine, but I think Mr. Rascliffe here isn't doing so well; looks like he just passed out!" I said while shrugging my shoulders. The guard nodded as he stared down at the limp and motionless body.

"Are you done with this piece of garbage?" he asked. The correctional officer lightly kicked at the crumpled and bruised figure on the cell floor.

"You can take him back now. Thanks again for your help." I lightly tapped the guard's shoulder with appreciation. As I left the prison, I felt a bit shaken at the fact that I had almost lost control of the situation which could have ended in disaster.

Maria was anxiously awaiting my return from the interrogation with James Rascliffe. I arrived at her house within the hour. Sparing no details, I gave her a full report, including the part about my horrendous error.

"We've already pulled the records from each of the pay phones," said Maria.

"Unfortunately, it seems the mystery woman had it set up so she couldn't be traced." Maria heaved a huge sigh. For a moment, something she had said struck me as odd.

"Hmmm…wait a minute! You can only use a pay phone to make a call; not to receive one." I remained quiet for a moment thinking I may have just hit on something rather important. Maria, on the hand, looked confused.

"Maria, the public phone system has been specifically set up for one-way calls excluding other pay phones. So if Rascliffe was telling the truth, he was calling back his contact using a pay phone. How was that possible?" I thought out loud.

"Someone on the inside had to of reroute the calls!" Maria began to catch on.

"I'll have Sherrie work on the pay phone business and see if it leads anywhere. Maybe we can use it to our advantage." Maria was busily taking down notes.

"It's going to be quite difficult to connect Rascliffe to Lena Harris and prove she was the one who ordered the murders, let alone tie her to the money affairs. We're talking about someone who worked on the Presidential staff for heaven's sake!" exclaimed Maria as worried lines pulled across her solemn face.

"Why don't you go home and try to get some rest, Alix." I agreed with Maria whole heartedly then headed back to my quiet and empty home. The evening commotion with Rascliffe left me physically and emotionally drained.

That night as I tossed and turned in my bed, an array of strange visions and endless tunnels raced around my head. I abruptly awoke soaked to the skin with perspiration as the glowing green numbers shouted 5:35 a.m. from my wooden night stand. It would seem I had only been asleep for a few hours.

I regretfully began to think about my upcoming trial and the unsettlement of a weak defense. The prosecution would try and discredit me, no doubt, and label me as an over zealous FBI agent who decided to go against protocol. Now, because of my lack of judgment and self control, I would have to account for killing Lena Harris who had worked for the President of the United States. And to make matters even worse, if convicted, I could spend the rest of my living days behind a set of metal bars without the hope of ever being free again.

CHAPTER 15

The next two weeks flew by and Maria could not find the slightest piece of evidence to connect Rascliffe to Lena Harris. Sherrie Frede, Maria's assistant and partner, was able to track down the origin of the wire transfer into Rascliffe's account. Unfortunately, it came from an overseas stockbroker's firm and finding out who pushed the button would take a considerable amount of time which we did not have. I knew her efforts would be futile, but I admired Sherrie's relentless determination.

In the early morning of the first day of my trial, I decided to go visit Sierra before heading to the courthouse. Sierra's condition had not changed. Thoughts of never being able to see her again rested heavy on my mind. Tears of sadness stained my cheeks and dropped endlessly upon her white clean sheets, but still Sierra remained oblivious of my fate.

By the time I reached the courthouse, I was somewhat composed as I placed myself next to Maria. She was dressed professionally in a thin pinstriped suit. Piles of papers were neatly stacked on the elongated red mahogany table. Sherrie Frede sat calmly on the other side of Maria. Their heads locked together as they busily reviewed the opening statement. Out in the hallway spectators had already lined up single file in order to get a reserved seat inside the stuffy courtroom. Within minutes, it was full to capacity and many people had to be turned away due to lack of space.

"Alix, how are you holding up?" whispered Maria. Regardless of their optimism, I felt isolated. My destiny now rested in the hands of twelve unknown people.

"I'm fine. Thank you for caring, Maria. I couldn't have done this without you and your wonderful friendship." My smile was sad, but sincere. I was truly grateful for Maria's dedication and her abundant wealth of knowledge of the legal system. With caring eyes, she gently squeezed my sweaty hand.

All at once, the side door in the courtroom opened. Twelve nameless jurors entered then filed in to their pre-assigned seats.

"All rise for the honorable Judge Patrick McHenry!" shouted the bailiff. The tall well built elderly judge strolled majestically in with a long black silky robe. Shock then despair covered my attorney's face. Maria leaned in close and whispered.

"I can't believe this! I was counting on Judge Cesseran!" Maria was more than just unhappy. She was outraged by this sudden unfortunate switch. The bailiff read the case number and the list of charges brought against me by the State of Ohio.

"We will begin with opening remarks. Mr. Santez, you may proceed." The judge cleared his throat as he peered over his wire-rimmed glasses at the prosecution. Maria had told me once about her good friend Elmino Santez, who now represented the prosecution for the State of Ohio. She also informed how Santez had drastically changed after he became a criminal defense attorney. His tactics turned dirty when he flipped to the other side. Other attorneys viewed his courtroom antics as unethical. Maria, in time, had lost all respect for him. Santez had just finished with the prosecution's opening statement.

"Ms. Shiner, you may proceed with your opening remarks." Judge Patrick McHenry's eyes never left his notepad as he busily kept writing. Maria forged on with her speech.

"…and Agent Alixandria Becker acted under the auspice of the Federal Bureau of Investigation and performed her duty as any other agent would have done…" Maria barely had started when the bailiff stepped up and handed Judge McHenry a folded piece of paper.

"The defense will continue with its opening statement after the court takes a brief recess." Judge McHenry quickly exited the courtroom. The jury was ushered into the holding room to wait for the trial to resume. Maria shook her head then sat down. A creeping grin crawled across the face of Santez as he eyed Maria up and down.

"Alix, I'm a little concerned over the fact Judge McHenry is ruling over this courtroom and not Judge Cesseran. McHenry and I, well, let's just say, he's not too fond of me." Maria shrugged her shoulders.

"He's not fond of you because you were the only one who had balls enough to question his decision in Tidious vs. Mastronni." Sherrie's voice was low and strong.

"What are you two talking about?" I asked. Sherrie continued on with pride.

"Maria found out through a highly reliable source that Judge Patrick McHenry was dirty! He had been taking bribes on the sly and then when it came to certain cases…well, you can just imagine, Alix!" exclaimed Sherrie.

"I wasn't even working on the Tidious-Mastronni case, but accidentally came upon the information about McHenry. The source was one of the best I ever worked with so I decided to do a little digging myself. I opened four of his cases he had made a ruling during the past two years that were definitely questionable. McHenry caught wind of what I was trying to do and stomped on my investigation. If you didn't already read about it in the newspaper, Judge McHenry is itching to fill a vacant seat as a Supreme Court Judge." Maria tapped her pencil on her notepad.

"You and I both know he's nothing but a sham!" Sherrie was furious.

"Well, unfortunately, it's not going to help us now. At least with Judge Cesseran, I had free rein in her courtroom," mumbled Maria with a concerned face. I felt a bit uncomfortable by her uneasiness.

Judge McHenry finally returned after about twenty minutes and the jury was escorted back into the courtroom. Maria proceeded then concluded with her opening remarks.

"Mr. Santez. You may call your first witness." Judge McHenry reached for his pen and pad of paper. The heavy back doors of the courtroom swung opened. The female witness sauntered down the center aisle. Her high heels clicked noisily on the floor. The bailiff was waiting for her as she reached the witness area.

"Hold up your right hand. Do you swear to tell the truth, the whole truth, and nothing but the truth?" asked the bailiff.

"I do," replied the witness. As she sat down in the witness box, her eyes held mine. I stared for a moment while I frantically wracked my brain as to where I had seen that face before. Maria immediately picked up on our direct eye contact.

"Do you know her?" whispered Maria. I thought I did for a moment, but my mind drew a blank.

"I'm not sure," I replied hesitantly.

"Please state your name for the record," asked the prosecution. Santez stood to the side of the witness stand patiently awaiting her response.

"Leslie Higgins," she replied in a loud voice. Santez placed his hands behind his back and paced slowly in front of the witness box.

"Ms. Higgins, are you employed?" he asked while looking down at the floor.

"Yes, I am the President of the Board of the Foundation for Greater Awareness for Women," she answered in a firm and confident tone.

"Can you tell us a little something about this board you serve on as president for the Greater Awareness for Women?" He moved to the side and faced the jury. Leslie Higgins was dressed in a dark red leather suit. Her skirt was extremely tight and short. It hugged and clung to her shapely hips and thighs. Her low cut blouse exposed tanned cleavage.

"The board serves as a liaison between well renowned businesses and their need to fill upper management positions. We act as a conduit between qualified women seeking a career in management supported fields and the various businesses in need of filling managerial positions." Higgins spoke directly to the jury.

"So, what you're saying is that you could be, well, let's say, a glorified employment agency?" Santez directed his question to the jury. Higgins' grin was weak.

"No. We are not a 'glorified' employment agency. We deal with top professional people and highly educational and motivated women who are seeking appropriate management positions." Higgins appeared to be agitated.

"I apologize, Ms. Higgins, excuse my ignorance. Let me rephrase my definition. This agency provides the opportunity for highly skilled and intelligent women to be placed in high paying jobs." Santez was smiling now. Leslie quickly looked away from Santez and shifted in her seat.

"What exactly are your functions as board president?" He rocked back and forth on the balls of his feet.

"I oversee the direction and function of the board. I approve the selection of the candidates which are recommended by the board as a whole." Higgins already appeared to be weary of Santez's insignificant questions.

"So, in other words, you make the final decision on who gets what job? Is this correct, Ms. Higgins?" Santez stepped back for a moment.

"Yes," she replied.

"That's a big responsibility, wouldn't you say, Ms. Higgins? You decide whether or not a certain woman is qualified for a certain position. You make the decision between, steak or eggs, if I may coin the term so loosely." His cocky smile was annoying.

"I wouldn't exactly use those words," she threw back. Santez completely ignored her sarcastic add on and continued with his questions.

"Have you ever not approved the selection of a candidate recommended by the board as a whole?" he asked. But before Leslie Higgins could respond, Maria abruptly stood up.

"I object your Honor to this line of questioning by Mr. Santez. It is immaterial and irrelevant to this case." Maria sat back down.

"Overruled counselor! If you haven't noticed, this is the prosecution's witness!" bellowed Judge McHenry.

"Mr. Santez, refine your questions and make your point. Ms. Shiner, I hope this isn't the beginning of your courtroom theatrics you had so adamantly demonstrated in my presence during previous trials. I will have no dramatics in this court! Is that understood, Ms. Shiner?" The elderly judge peered down at Maria as she stood up to respond.

"Yes, your Honor, understood." Maria was cut off immediately.

"Sit down counselor, now!" Judge McHenry shook his head in defiance. I could have sworn that McHenry had just called Maria a vile name under his breath. Maria dropped down heavily onto the wooden chair. She was fuming. It hadn't even been an hour into the trial and already Judge McHenry was making it difficult for Maria. Santez gloated nearby.

"Ms. Higgins, you are to answer the question." Judge McHenry looked once again at Maria. Maria immediately broke eye contact and looked at her notes.

"Could you please repeat the question?" Higgins asked reluctantly.

"Certainly, I would like to know if you ever disagreed with the choice candidate that was recommended by the entire board at any time?" repeated Santez.

"Yes, there have been several candidates, at one time or another, I felt were not qualified and decided against the board's recommendations." Her words were sharp and filled with authority.

"Ms. Higgins, how many women have you placed, oh let's say, within a one month period?" Santez seemed to be dragging his feet on purpose.

"Well, our organization is very popular and well renowned; it all depends. We service the entire country, but our main office is based here in Ohio. Placement may range between 10-20 women a month." She seemed satisfied with her answer.

"That's very impressive. If I may ask, where do you receive your funds to finance such a national operation as this?" Santez reached the jury box.

"Each woman pays an initial set-up fee when they complete an application. After a rigorous screening process, they are placed on a waiting list to be matched against various opened positions. Once hired, a portion of their salary is sent to us during the first year of employment. We also accept private donations from those who believe in our cause." Higgins studied her lines well.

"Hmmm, okay. How much is the initial set-up fee?" He continued on with his questioning.

"The initial fee with the application is based on the qualifications and skills of the certain individual. The range of fees begin at a minimum of $1,000 to a maximum of $5,000," she stated.

"And what is the percentage taken out of the individual's salary for the first year?" Santez stood still for a moment while she answered.

"It usually comes out to be roughly 25% of their base salary." Higgins cleared her throat.

"Hefty sum of money, wouldn't you say, Ms. Higgins?" he asked quizzically.

"Not really, when you think of the positions these women will hold. Their salaries could range from $150,000 to well over $200,000 a year. So a $1,000 application fee and 25% for the first year, well, no; it's a small price to pay for success." She looked taken back by his insinuation. Maria was once again becoming restless over the purpose of this witness and the direction of questioning.

"How long has your organization been in business?" asked Santez smiling.

"It was initially started by a local business woman almost twenty years ago. It grew to be a nationwide enterprise, mainly in support of women's rights for equal employment." Higgins shifted in her chair. Santez walked over to his table and lifted his white pad of paper.

"Did a woman by the name of Lena Harris ever come to your organization seeking help for employment prospects?" he queried.

"Yes," she replied curtly.

"So you were able to place Lena Harris?" quizzed Santez.

"You have to understand that sometimes it can take up to a year, if not more, before we find the best possible employment match for each individual's skills. If I remember correctly, Lena Harris did not want to wait and joined the military service." Santez rubbed his chin as he shook his head in agreement.

"Did she ever come back to your organization after she left the military?" continued Santez.

"Yes, she did." Higgins seemed to be on edge with the length of her questioning.

"And were you able to help her the second time?" questioned Santez.

"Yes." Higgins once again shifted in her seat, but this time she tugged at her leather tight skirt. As the questions continued on, I closed my eyes and tried to focus on the voice of Leslie Higgins.

"What type of employment, in your opinion, suited with the skills of Lena Harris?" Santez threw Maria a side glance. Maria ignored his glare and sat back in her chair. She then slowly tapped her pencil on the yellow pad.

"Lena Harris had an extensive and highly notable background with the military. We arranged for an interview for a position as a member on the White House staff." Higgins scratched her neck.

"So you're saying it is your organization that got Ms. Harris her job at the White House?" Santez moved a bit further back from the witness box.

"What I'm saying is that our organization provided her with the means and opportunity for an interview. It was Lena's high security level, impeccable and unblemished background, and her impressive military accomplishments that got her the job. As they say, you're only as good as the product you sell," Higgins stated firmly.

"Did you have any contact with Ms. Harris after she became a member on the White House staff?" Higgins waited a brief moment before answering.

"No, once she moved to Washington D.C., I never saw her again." Leslie Higgins seemed a bit nervous.

"Ms. Higgins, we can safely say your only contact with Ms. Harris was strictly in connection to finding her a suitable position of employment through resources provided by your organization," stated Santez.

"Yes." Higgins dramatically bowed her head.

"Thank you, Ms. Higgins. Your honor, I have no further questions for this witness at this time." Judge McHenry nodded.

"The defense may cross examine Ms. Higgins at this time." Judge McHenry looked bored.

"Thank you, your Honor." Maria moved slowly toward the witness stand.

"Ms. Higgins, you mentioned in your testimony here today that you serve women across the entire United States. Is this correct?" asked Maria.

"Yes," she replied.

"Ms. Higgins, just to set the record straight, you also stated that your placement of individuals can range from 10-20 a month if not more or less. Is this correct?" pressed Maria. Higgins looked a bit baffled by Maria's questions.

"Yes," she answered.

"Hmmmm…that would make a total of at least 120 women a year or more. So, how is it that you could remember so easily, without hesitating even for a moment, a woman by the name of Lena Harris?" Maria stepped back with folded arms. And before Higgins could even respond, Maria jumped back with yet another question.

"Can you name five of the women you placed two years ago?" Higgins looked flustered by Maria's underlying accusation and did not answer.

"How about two or three? Let's say, three women from Arizona." Maria was on a roll, but it was short lived.

"I object, your Honor! The defense is badgering the witness with questions! And Ms. Higgins' memory is not on trial!" shouted Santez.

"Sustained; counselor, what is the point of this questioning?" Judge McHenry appeared to be aggravated.

"Your Honor, I am trying to show that Ms. Higgins' recollection of…" Maria was just getting started when she was cut off rudely by McHenry.

"Counselor, approach the bench," commanded the judge. Santez grinned from ear-to-ear at Maria's misgivings. He knew he had the case wrapped up and sealed even before it started.

"Ms. Shiner, either get to the point or release this witness. I know where you are heading with this, counselor, and I don't like it at all. You're grasping at straws and trying to connect Higgins and Harris to the murder case. There is no relevancy here whatsoever! Move on or let her go!" His voice was stern and projecting. Maria backed away and was fuming.

"Yes, your Honor." Maria cleared her throat and started from the beginning with Leslie Higgins.

"Ms. Higgins, out of all the women you place each year, why is it you remember Lena Harris?" asked Maria. Leslie Higgins remained silent for a moment. She quickly glanced at Santez.

"There are many candidates that stand out from the others. Lena Harris was more than exceptional. She held unique qualities that some women could only dream of but instead she used them to her advantage. She became a prestigious member on the White House Staff." Higgins was more than satisfied with her answer.

"So, let me paraphrase your answer. You remember Lena Harris because your agency was able to supply her with the resources she needed to land the job at the White House." Maria slowed her pace and stopped in front of the jury box.

"You could say it that way to make things a little easier to understand." Higgins slowly nodded her head in agreement. Maria walked over to our table and picked up a sheet of paper. She remained silent for only a second.

"Have you ever helped place any other women, other than Lena Harris, inside the White House?" Maria had something slick up her sleeve. Higgins shifted nervously in her seat as her cheeks became slightly flushed.

"Well, I guess... I would have to review my files back at the office." Higgins stared up at the judge.

"You would have to review your files? If your agency had helped place others in the White House, why would you single out remembering only Lena Harris?" Maria was back on her feet only to be prematurely shut down.

"Counselor, I warned you about this line of questioning! I will not tolerate your contempt to my rulings!" Judge McHenry slammed down his gavel.

"Ms. Higgins, you may step down out of the witness box." Leslie Higgins quickly slid out of the hot seat and walked swiftly from the courtroom.

"Your Honor! You cannot dismiss my witness..." The entire courtroom was in an uproar. McHenry continued to slam his gavel over and over until silence filled the air.

"I will deal with you privately in my chambers, Ms. Shiner. The jury will disregard the questions by the Defense and the testimony given by Leslie Higgins in response. The jury is dismissed until tomorrow morning at 9 a.m." McHenry was on the war path.

"All rise," called out the bailiff. Judge McHenry exited the courtroom in a rush. The murmur of voices dissipated as onlookers shuffled out.

"I have to go see him!" Maria, in a huff, gathered her notes and then roughly shoved them all inside her worn briefcase. I stood alone with Sherrie. Disappointment covered her face.

"It doesn't look good, Alix. McHenry is doing everything possible to make you look guilty. He just won't let up on Maria." But much to our surprise Maria reappeared after only been gone a few minutes.

"He had a change of heart. I get one more shot at Higgins tomorrow. I can recall her if I want as long as I don't pursue the same line of questioning." Maria looked a bit relieved.

"Maria, we all know there's a definite connection between Higgins and Harris. I think that Higgins recruited members for Lena's group of vigilante wannabes," summarized Sherrie. I completely agreed with Sherrie. The Greater Awareness for Women agency would be the perfect cover up. Where else could you find such women who held power and distinction then those who were placed in prominent positions through the agency?

The following day came with a seasonal mix of rain and snow. The courtroom was chilly and damp. It wasn't long before it was filled with curious spectators. Leslie Higgins was not pleased at the fact she had to return back to the witness stand.

"Ms. Higgins, from your testimony yesterday, I think we all agree that it has been established you have the utmost authority when it comes down to matching candidates to employment. Could you please take a look at this list of names, Ms. Higgins?" Maria handed Leslie Higgins a typed piece of paper. The courtroom was still as Higgins eyed the names suspiciously.

"Now, to the best of your recollection, do any of names look familiar to you?" Maria pressed on. Suddenly, small beads of sweat began to form along her hairline.

"No, not off hand." Higgins shoved the list back to Maria.

"Look again, Ms. Higgins. There are 12 names on the list. Did any of these women ever seek help from your agency for employment placement?" Higgins' eyes darted to Santez who was already squirming in his seat.

"Ms. Higgins, should I repeat the question?" asked Maria with a slight grin.

"I would have to consult my files," she replied hastily.

"You mean you don't recognize a single name on the list?" pushed Maria.

"I already…told you…no!" she stammered.

"Please, Ms. Higgins, look again." Maria was confident.

"Why do you keep badgering me? I said there is not one name on this list that I recognize!" Higgins tone rose as she became flustered by Maria's insistence.

"And what does this have to do with the agency?" Higgins tossed the sheet of paper over the railing onto the courtroom floor. Maria stood back and watched as Leslie Higgins unraveled and lost control.

"I know what you're trying to do, counselor, and…and you think you're smart, but there isn't any connection…I'm done with this!" Suddenly, Leslie

Higgins jumped up and began to remove herself from the witness stand. Judge McHenry threw Santez a dirty look. A loud mumbling of voices erupted throughout the courtroom.

"Ms. Higgins! Please return to the witness seat! You will answer the question. I will instruct you when it is time to step down. Is that understood?" McHenry was standing up now and glaring down at Higgins. Higgins was visibly shaken by the whole ordeal. The hefty bailiff already had Higgins' arm and was escorting her back to the witness stand. Suddenly, her delicate poise turned into a set of jangled nerves. Maria graciously, once again, handed the list to Higgins.

"Ms. Higgins, I ask you once again to look at this list of names. Do you recognize any of the names on this list?" queried Maria. Higgins took a deep breath before answering. She closed her eyes and tried desperately to gather her composure.

"No," she responded with confidence.

"Let the records reflect that Exhibit B-5 is the list of names of women who did indeed use the services of Greater Awareness for Women and were found murdered within the last year." Maria had just hit a home run! The courtroom went wild. McHenry was furious as he smashed his intimidating tool over and over again.

"I object your Honor! This line of questioning is argumentative! Ms. Shiner is insinuating that there is a connection between the women who were murdered to the organization in which Ms. Higgins is employed!" shouted Santez.

"Your Honor! How can Mr. Santez object to evidence submitted and reviewed by both sides? I am merely stating a fact. The twelve women on this list were placed for employment through the Greater Awareness for Women agency *and* have been found murdered within the last year! How can you object to the facts?" questioned Maria while throwing up her arms in front of the jury box.

"Sustained! Mr. Santez maybe you should have paid closer attention to the evidence in submission," hissed Judge McHenry. He had no choice but to rule in favor of Maria.

"Ms. Higgins, don't you find it rather odd that these twelve women who asked your agency for help to find employment are now dead?" Maria's tone was quite forceful. The courtroom, once again, buzzed with voices.

"I will have silence in my courtroom!" Judge McHenry shouted. Higgins did not know how to respond. She frantically glared at Santez for help.

"Ms. Higgins, you must answer the question," McHenry stated reluctantly.

"I plead the fifth!" Higgins announced with vengeance. The courtroom was awestruck by Leslie Higgins outburst.

"Bailiff, escort the witness out of the courtroom. Court is recessed until 9 a.m. tomorrow morning." The courtroom dramatics had ended early for the day.

"All rise," shouted the bailiff. The jury was escorted from their seats through a side exit. Judge McHenry disappeared into his chambers. Spectators slowly filed out of the overfilled courtroom. The three of us sat at the table in silence. It was still mid morning and my stomach felt empty.

"I could go for a bite to eat," exclaimed Sherrie. Both Maria and I nodded in agreement.

The Italian restaurant across the street from City Hall was quiet and held few customers. After all three of us finished indulging on an early lunch, we discussed the courtroom stage show.

"Maria, I was so impressed with the way you blew Higgins testimony straight out the window!" I exclaimed. Maria smiled then held her diet Pepsi up high.

"One for the good girls!" she shouted. We all clanked glasses and began to chuckle.

"Did you see Higgins' face when she read the list of names?" asked Sherrie as she munched on the small bowl of nuts.

"What was even more amusing was the fact McHenry's hands were tied and he couldn't do a damn thing about it!" We all roared with laughter.

"Well, if that doesn't prove to the jury there is a definite connection between Higgins and Harris..." Sherrie did not bother to finish her sentence. Instead, she cupped another handful of nuts and tossed them freely into her mouth.

"Maria, I know you don't want to hear this but..." And before I could finish, Maria held up her hand in protest.

"Alix, no!" she stated firmly. Maria knew exactly where I was heading and wanted me to change directions.

"Maria, maybe Alix is right." Sherrie shrugged her shoulders.

"Whose side are you on anyway, Sherrie! Alix, you know how I feel about you taking the stand in your own defense! I don't recommend it at all!" Maria was busily sipping her soda from the frosty glass.

"Why? This way everyone would know the truth!" I protested.

"I know Higgins was there that night! She was one of Lena's henchwomen who brutalized Sierra!" Fury began to build at the recap of that never ending nightmare.

"No, Alix! The prosecution will literally rip your testimony to shreds and shove it down your throat until you choke!" Maria looked drained.

"I've had enough; I want to wake up for court tomorrow." Maria yawned then leaned slightly into Sherrie.

"Why counselor, I'd say you look a wee bit tired!" Sherrie snickered.

"I'm haven't been sleeping too well and I still have some work to go over after we get home." Maria snatched the check from my hand.

"See you in the morning, Alix!" shouted Maria and Sherrie in unison as they headed for their Jaguar. I sat by myself for a moment after the two of them had left. All of a sudden, my eyes felt extremely heavy. I thought of Sierra and how her fate rested on her will to survive. There was nothing medically that could be done. Right now, Sierra lived in her own world of solace, away from all the misgivings and the trial, away from all her friends, and worst of all, the most disheartening, away from me.

CHAPTER 16

Once again, the courtroom overflowed with curious onlookers and media. Judge Patrick McHenry was considerably late. Tension rose and filled the atmosphere as time gradually ticked away.

"All rise for the Honorable Judge Patrick McHenry presiding!" shouted the bald and extremely overweight bailiff. The whole courtroom stood to attention. The jury was issued in one by one.

"The prosecution may continue; please call your next witness." Judge McHenry had been busily jotting down something on his legal pad.

"Thank you, your Honor." Santez called three more witnesses. It was late afternoon when McHenry called it a day. We were about to leave when the bailiff handed Maria a folded note. It was from Judge McHenry requesting her presence in his chamber.

"Go on ahead without me; I'll catch up, later." Maria grabbed her brown leather bag and headed for the backroom. Sherrie and I decided to make our way to the family owned deli located a block down the street from City Hall. It wasn't long before Maria joined the group.

"Can you believe the gall of Santez and his ridiculous offer?" she exclaimed.

"He wanted you to plea guilty to second-degree murder with a reduced sentence of serving not less than 25 years! What a joke!" Maria threw her hands up in the air.

"So I take it you told him to stuff it?" I asked.

"Well, to put it nicely. I told him that we 'declined' the State's offer at this time. Then as we walked out of the court house, I told him to shove his offer straight up his ass and choke on it!" Maria slammed her hand down on the table with such force the silverware rattled in protest. Sherrie and I burst into laughter. Maria's rough edges were surpassed by her humorous ability to deal with confrontation and harsh reality. As the laughter died down, silence consumed the table.

"Do I have a chance Maria? Please tell me the truth?" Worried lines creased across Maria's forehead.

"Alix, the jury has been instructed to follow the law. And the law states you are innocent until proven guilty. The prosecution has to show you were guilty of the crimes charged against you. My job is to show that the actions taken by you were warranted and that there were no crimes committed. And if we are able to drag in Lena Harris' dirty laundry…well, so be it!" Maria seemed confident and had faith in the justice system.

The evening hour approached quickly as we finished our dinner. Tomorrow was a new day in court and no one knew what to expect. Santez was out for blood, and unfortunately, it was mine.

The following two days in court were repetitively the same. The prosecution had finished with all its witnesses and now it was time for the defense. Judge McHenry ended court early Friday afternoon. The defense would start the following week with their line of questioning first thing on Monday morning.

In the back of my mind, the need to take the stand in my own defense kept inching itself forward to the surface. Once again, after voicing my concerns, Maria insisted on discrediting my illusion of being forthright. I could not understand how explaining to the jury what really happened could jeopardize my already pending doom. Maria had given up all hope on Sierra's miraculous recovery. I, too, doubted in the powers above and the merciful hand that could reignite the life that had been long lost in the loving eyes of Sierra.

We worked diligently over the weekend to prepare for Monday morning in court. Our plan of defense included character witnesses on my behalf. They were to show my stability and accredited background I had encompassed during my tenure at the FBI. Maria's aim was to portray me as someone who could not possibly be a cold hearted killer, but a dedicated agent with exceptional intuitive training skills.

Monday morning came shortly along with its down falls. It didn't take long before McHenry was at it again, cutting Maria down where she stood. But as Maria struggled to fight her own battle against McHenry's threats of contempt, I felt my freedom quickly slipping away.

"Sherrie, we still need to somehow link the Greater Awareness for Women Organization to the list of murdered women. I know if I call Higgins back to the stand, McHenry will figure out my intentions and shoot down my whole line of questioning. We just have to figure out how to introduce it in court without ticking off McHenry," whispered Maria.

"May I approach the bench, your Honor?" requested Maria. McHenry's eyebrow darted up.

"You may approach the bench; the both of you!" allowed McHenry.

"Your Honor how am I to question my witnesses when Mr. Santez objects to every remark or question I present?" Judge McHenry stopped writing and stared hard at Maria.

"I object your Honor to this verbal attack!" Santez whispered harshly. McHenry's patience had worn thin.

"Ms. Shiner, need I remind you about your show of theatrics in my courtroom!" Maria let out a huge sigh while Santez skirted himself behind Maria.

"You're in contempt counselor and I will not have any more of this kind of performance in my courtroom. Do you understand?" He covered his mike as he peered down upon both parties.

"Yes, your Honor, I understand." Maria barely made eye contact with the scheming judge.

"Good. Ms. Shiner, you are fined $500 dollars and then maybe next time you'll think twice before opening that big mouth of yours!" Maria was infuriated. She bit her lower lip as she returned to the table.

"The witness will step down and the Defense will continue with its questioning of the witness tomorrow at 9:00 a.m. The jury is dismissed." McHenry grabbed his notepad and disappeared from the courtroom without waiting for the announcement from the bailiff.

"I don't understand why we just can't tell the jury about how the White House is involved in a major cover up!" I felt the need to vent my mounting frustrations.

"You can tell any kind of story you want, but without proof, well, as you can see for yourself, Alix, it doesn't hold a candle in the water. It doesn't matter which approach I take, I keep hitting a brick wall and he is called McHenry! Unfortunately, he controls the courtroom." Maria rubbed her burning eyes. Just then a young courier rushed in and stood anxiously in front of Maria.

"Are you Maria Shiner?" he asked.

"Yes, I am," she responded curiously. He handed her a large brown envelope and asked for a signature. It was labeled "Evidence" in bold letters.

"What in the name of..." Maria's voice trailed off into silence as she pulled out the letter.

"This is outrageous!" she shouted with desperation.

"Sherrie, feast your eyes on this!" Maria handed Sherrie the packet of papers. Sherrie's eyes were wide with disbelief.

"Santez is going to have a field day with this piece of trumped up evidence." Cynicism covered Maria's face.

"What is it?" I asked while my heart skipped a beat at the thought of yet another nail slamming in to seal my fate.

"It states that Lena Harris was on a highly secretive operation to infiltrate a congregation of women who were thought to be responsible for numerous deaths including government officials." Sherrie need not read on. I knew exactly what this meant for me.

"I know you don't want to hear this again, Maria, but I want to take the stand!" My voice was firm. Sherrie and Maria looked at one another in despair.

"I don't think it will make much of difference, now, Maria. At least let Alix say her peace," mumbled Sherrie. Maria finally gave in and nodded in agreement.

"At least if I am to go down for what I believe in, I want everyone, especially the jury and media, to hear my side of the story! I would like all of them to hear the truth! Hopefully, with a lot of luck and an over abundance of prayers, the jury will come to their senses and see that I am innocent." I swallowed hard as a knot formed within my dry throat.

"And if they don't, I guess I'm in for the ride of my life." We all looked at one another and unfortunately came to the same devastating conclusion.

"I really admire you, Alix. Your outlook on everything still seems to be relatively positive considering…" Sherrie did not bother to finish. I knew in my heart and my mind, that my actions on that fatal day were warranted and necessary to save Sierra's life and my own.

The following day was yet another cold and dreary day and it began as each previous day. Santez glowed with glory as he displayed the vital piece of evidence that would eventually bring me full term.

"Your Honor, I would like to call Alixandria Becker to the witness stand." Maria's half-grin and nod led me to believe my notable intentions were approved.

"Please hold up your right hand. Do you swear to tell the whole truth and nothing but the truth?" asked the bailiff.

"I do." Butterflies raced up and down inside my stomach. I could feel the eyes of so many as I sat in the spotlight before the entire courtroom.

"Please state your full name for the court records." Maria stuck to formality.

"Alixandria Becker," I replied.

"Ms. Becker, could you please tell the court and the jury where you are employed?" She strolled in front of the witness box as I explained my occupation.

"Ms. Becker, could you explain to the court why you requested to take the stand in your own defense after I, insisted as your attorney, against such actions?" Maria's approach was simple. Maybe using a slight touch of reverse psychology couldn't hurt. I cleared my throat and took a deep breath.

"I want the court to know the absolute truth about what really happened and why I did what I believed I had a duty to do." Maria tossed me a quick wink.

"Ms. Becker, could you please, in your own words, describe in detail, to the jury and the court, the events which led up to the night you killed Special Agent Lena Harris." Maria went back and sat down behind the long wooden table. The courtroom grew uncomfortably quiet as I began my unrehearsed testimony. After two short breaks and several glasses of water, I finally reached the most important part leading up to the incident with Lena Harris. Santez sat unusually still as he hurriedly jotted down notes. I anxiously emphasized the fact that both of our lives were threatened and in grave danger warranting the use of extreme force to remedy the inevitable explosive situation.

"Thank you for your testimony, Ms. Becker." Maria nodded in approval.

"You may cross examine the witness, Mr. Santez." Judge McHenry had removed his glasses and sat back relaxed within his cushioned chair. Santez slowly stood and walked lazily toward me with a sheet of paper in his hand.

"Alixandria Becker, or should I say, formerly Agent Alixandria Becker?" he asked.

"I'm confused by your question, is there one?" The jury giggled at his ineptness and lack of clarification.

"Are you an agent as we speak?" he snapped.

"I was put on Administrative Leave without pay pending the outcome of this trial." My response was tight.

"So, may I safely say, you are no longer an FBI agent?" My silence fed fuel to the fire.

"Ms. Becker, I am assuming by your silence, you are in agreement?" Santez paced the floor in front of the witness box. Without waiting for my answer, he continued on.

"Let's go back to the part of your testimony when you trespassed onto private property." Santez was on a roll.

"Objection, your Honor! Pure speculation, referring that my client was trespassing has no relevancy." Maria was on her feet.

"Sustained! Counselor, leave your antiquated surmising techniques for another courtroom. Let's move it along, please." Judge McHenry looked bored.

"Ms. Becker, let's go back to the part in your testimony when you entered the premises on the assumption of looking for evidence related to the murder case you were assigned to work on with Special Agent Sierra Montgomery. Once you gained illegal access inside, you and Special Agent Montgomery discovered an organization of women who were dressed in leather attire and had just made plans on taking over the world."

"I object your Honor!" shouted Maria. Within that split second, the entire courtroom burst out into laughter. Judge McHenry was furious! He continuously slammed down his gavel until the hoots of merriment subsided. Suddenly, my cheeks felt hot as my face flushed with embarrassment. Santez was right. The story sounded ludicrous to any person with half a mind. What was I thinking? As Maria so predicted it came true; I could feel myself choking on my own words.

"Mr. Santez! I *will not* tolerate this show of theatrical performances by the prosecution! This is not a comedy club! This is a court of law! I will hold you in contempt the next time you even think about using my courtroom as a laughing gallery! Do you understand me, counselor?" Judge McHenry shouted heatedly. Perspiration formed along Santez's brow.

"Yes, your Honor." Santez glared at Maria.

"Do you like to read fiction books, Ms. Becker?" asked Santez. Surprised by the change in questioning, it took me a moment before I could respond.

"Ms. Becker, a simple yes or no will do. Do you like to read fiction books?" He walked lazily to the front of the witness stand.

"I suppose I do." I looked helplessly at Maria. Maria held back to see what Santez was up to with this outlandish line of questioning.

"Could it be, due to the immense amount of stress from your overload of work at the FBI, that you unconsciously incorporated fact with fiction in regards to the secret cult of women in leather?" A buzz of giggles erupted throughout the courtroom.

"I object your Honor! This line of questioning is irrelevant and immaterial!" Maria was once again back on her feet.

"Counselor, I will not warn you again! Get to the point!" scolded McHenry. Santez gave a slight bow.

"Did you ever have sex with Special Agent Montgomery?" Santez suddenly tossed out a bomb.

"I strongly object, your Honor! Ms. Becker's sexuality is not on trial here!" voiced Maria.

"Your Honor, I am trying to show the deep bond shared between Ms. Becker and Special Agent Montgomery!" insisted Santez.

"Sustained! But don't dabble around, counselor, make your point!" McHenry's lip went up as his eyes narrowed at Santez's victory. Maria filled with fury, moved to approach the bench, but was suddenly cutoff by Sherrie. She nodded her head in disagreement.

"Ms. Becker, shall I repeat the question?" Santez gloated with animosity.

"No, I remember the question quite well. Yes, I have had sex with Special Agent Montgomery and to already answer your next question, yes, I am in love with her, too!" This time I felt a twinge of victory. The courtroom buzzed with excitement.

"My, my, Ms. Becker, now you can read minds? Nevertheless, the fact is *you* killed Special Agent Lena Harris!" He abruptly stopped pacing.

"Why did you kill Special Agent Lena Harris? Was it because she had an affair with your girlfriend, Sierra Montgomery, at one time and you wanted to get rid of any competition?" His question was absurd and quite ridiculous. Maria's chin rested on her chest.

"I killed Lena Harris because she threatened my life and that of Special Agent Sierra Montgomery." I stood firm with conviction.

"According to Exhibit 6-D, which I am sure defense has had ample time to review, it states Special Agent Lena Harris was indeed working undercover in an organization which consisted of powerful and politically based women." Santez stewed on his next sentence.

"Why would you automatically assume that Lena Harris had been persuaded to join the other side and betray her country? Then...take it upon yourself to rectify the situation by ending her life." I felt frustrated and indecisive.

"No, you've got it all wrong, that's not how it happened at all!" I stammered.

"Ms. Becker would you like me to repeat the question?" he persisted.

"No, I heard you the first time," I replied stalling for a moment to gather my shaky composure. The room filled with an eerie silence.

"Ms. Becker, you must answer the question or you will be held in contempt of court," sounded Judge McHenry. I looked at Sherrie then Maria for some type of guidance; but I knew I was on my own.

"I don't know," I said in a low tone.

"Could you please repeat your answer, Ms. Becker?" pushed Santez knowing full well what I had just replied.

"I don't know," I repeated out loud.

"You don't know? You don't know *why* you mercilessly snuffed out the life of an upstanding and respected woman who struggled aimlessly to overcome numerous obstacles to make her way and hold a prestigious position on the White House staff?" Santez backed away to let my peers gaze directly upon me. A couple of the jury members just shook their heads with disgust. The impending doom hit me hard as it sunk in deep within my soul. Not only had I lost Sierra to an unknown world beyond conscious reality, but now inside this courtroom within an instant, I knew it was over for me and nothing mattered anymore.

How do you explain the saturated feeling of fear to those who choose to live in a glass bottle? How do you explain the deterioration of hope for survival? How do you explain the fight against the evitable to which fate follows so close behind with no room for ultimate salvation? Solemnly, with dispiriting will and loss of conviction, I had found the answers.

Maria folded her hands then rested them on the table. She too, knew that my chance at freedom had been snatched away by just one small question. It gave the jurors exactly what they needed to decide my fate.

"No further questions, your Honor." Santez went back to his table and sat down.

"Are there any other witnesses you would like to call Ms. Shiner?" asked Judge McHenry.

"No, your Honor, the defense rests." Maria sighed heavily.

"You may step down now, Ms. Becker." Judge McHenry adjusted his bifocals.

"We will adjourn for the evening and resume in the morning with closing statements." A slam of his gavel ended yet another hopeless chapter in court.

Maria and Sherrie remained silent as we made our way through the underground parking garage. I had no appetite and wanted to be left alone. Maria had been right. She tried to warn me, but I wouldn't listen. Santez turned my testimony around and shoved it right down my throat and now I would choke on it all the way to prison.

CHAPTER 17

Another restless night entailed me as I tumbled into the unfitting darkness beyond the realms of a fitful night's sleep.

The wind was brisk as its icy fingers lightly touched my unprotected arms. My feet felt frozen to the ground. I could not move. I shivered from the intense cold. My chest heaved from emptiness and loneliness. How I longed for Sierra.

The alarm went off and I remained still as I stared dreamily up at the white ceiling of my bedroom. I knew this would be the last day I would spend in my own home. We all parted in good company the night before without discussing anything about the trial. Maria and Sherrie had done everything humanly possible for me. Today, a jury of my peers would decide on how I would be living the remainder of my life. Hopefully, but doubtfully, justice would prevail.

The courtroom, once again, was packed beyond seating capacity. Several television crews patiently waited outside the courtroom for the verdict. Judge McHenry was announced then seated as the jury was brought in to hear the closing arguments.

I sadly had to admit that Elmino Santez was brilliant. If I was one of the jurors, after hearing his moving speech, would cast my vote of "guilty" without doubt or hesitation. Maria, on the other hand, stressed the facts. She focused on my willingness to testify and reminded the jury that I was innocent and that the burden of proof was left up to the prosecution. She also emphasized the fact that even if Lena Harris was indeed undercover, it did not give her the right to jeopardize the lives of other agents. I was impressed by her fortitude and perseverance.

The jury was then escorted from the courtroom to deliberate their verdict. I had a strange feeling it would not take them very long. We sat in silence at the table. Santez was laughing and joking with his team. A rumble of voices could be heard throughout the stuffy courtroom as we all waited in anticipation of what would be my last day of freedom. After about an hour and a half of deliberation, the jury was escorted back into the courtroom to read its verdict.

"Have you reached a verdict?" asked Judge Patrick McHenry. By now, the three of us were standing tall.

"Yes, your Honor we have." The bailiff handed the small piece of note paper to the judge. He nodded and it was returned to the jury foreman.

"We the jury finds Alixandria Becker, guilty of first degree murder. We suggest life in prison without possibility of parole." Maria's hand tightened around mine. For a brief moment, it was if the wind had been knocked out of me. At that moment in time, my thoughts raced to Sierra. I couldn't hold back the tears of despair as I thought of our lost love ordained to be forgotten, not by will, but by choice. My eyes closed as my chin dropped unto my chest. The courtroom erupted in loud voices.

"Silence!" shouted McHenry as he pounded the gavel.

"Sentencing will be set two weeks from today. Bailiff, escort the prisoner out of the courtroom." The pudgy bailiff snapped the cuffs roughly around my wrists.

"We'll appeal, Alix, I won't give up until you're free!" exclaimed Maria. Sherrie was visibly shaken by this traumatic error in judgment. The bailiff grabbed my elbow and led me into a small holding cell where I would wait until I was sent to a prison facility. It didn't take long before my ride to my new home had arrived.

"Alixandria Becker?" A middle aged, medium built, rough looking woman stood before the iron door. Not standing much taller than I, her wide behind and large hips swished as she entered the holding cell.

"In the flesh!" I responded trying desperately to keep a positive outlook.

"Oh, so we have another comedian on our hands. We'll see how much you laugh when you get to where you're going!" With brute strength she roughly grabbed my arm and yanked me off the bench. The smell of rotten fish and sweat reeked from her dirty uniform.

"You don't have to be so rough!" I exclaimed. She snorted as she laughed exposing her badly crooked and overlapping teeth.

"I deal with pansies like you every single day. You're no different from them. You think because you were a big wig FBI agent, I give a horse's ass? You're in *my* world now, and you'll play by *my* rules. Got it?" She shoved me along until we reached a private cell with a solid metal door.

"Get in!" she yelled. I tripped then fell as she thrust me through the opening. She leaned over and unlocked my cuffs.

"Take your clothes off and put this on!" She lifted the orange suit from the wooden table and threw it in my face.

"And hurry up! I don't have all day!" Her greasy smile gave me the creeps. I could feel the weight of her heavy stare as I struggled with the unattractive prison garb.

"You're not too bad looking for a white piece of meat. I prefer my meat just a tad darker, know what I'm saying?" She eyed me up and down.

"I bet you do," I mumbled to myself.

"What'd you say to me?" She kicked my calf with full force. Searing pain radiated straight up into my thigh.

"We don't have all damn day!" Impatiently, she ripped at my silk blouse. Buttons scattered everywhere across the cell room floor.

"That's more like it." Suddenly by surprise, she grappled my right breast with her manly left hand. I instinctively pushed away from her touch holding back my instincts of responding with a full front kick to the groin. Beads of sweat stuck to her top hairy lip.

"Nice tits!" She proceeded once again to try and touch my body.

"Get your stinking hands off of me!" I cried. Within a second, the back of her hand hit me hard across my unprotected face. I fell to the floor as the warm ooze seeped from the side of my mouth.

"Oh, boo, hoo, the precious little FBI agent has got a fat lip. You'll learn real quick who's the boss in here!" Spittle fell on my bare arm as it seeped through her front yellow stained teeth.

"You got it mama's baby?" She grasped my hair in her hand then pulled back with might.

"Yeah, I got it," I said in almost a whisper.

"Got what? Say it so I can hear it!" she threatened.

"I got it!" I angrily shouted. Within a second she released her tearing hold on my hair.

"You belong to me cunt! My name is Roste. Lauren Roste. But you can call me sweet mama!" Unexpectedly, without any warning, she tried to kiss me sloppily on the lips. The smell of her breath almost made me vomit.

"There's plenty more where that came from, baby!" cackled Roste.

"Let's move out!" She put the handcuffs back into place along with shackles around my ankles. It made walking quite cumbersome as I tripped haphazardly along the hallway out to my awaited escort. The cuffs around my wrists and ankles dug in deep with each step. As I sat alone in the back of the paddy wagon, my thoughts, once again, turned to Sierra. I tried so hard to keep my emotions in tack avoiding an even bigger scene once I reached the prison. With determined focus of my mind, I was able to place myself within a deep trance of nonexistence.

"Wake up sleeping beauty!" Roste's voice startled me. I looked out of the back of the vehicle and saw the rest of my life before me. A thick metal fence topped off with cutting barbwire surrounded the elongated building. On the outside, each window was covered by solid steel bars. Positioned opposite of one another sat two large watchtowers that balanced out the odd shaped correctional facility. An enormous fenced-in activity area, with tennis nets and basketball hoops, had been strategically situated on a solid concrete pad near the east side of the building.

"Welcome home!" cried Roste. She viciously yanked at my cuffs causing me to lose my balance and fall heavily to the graveled ground.

"Hey, Roste, looks like she's head over heels for you already!" Several of the women correctional officers hooted out in unison.

"Get up, baby!" Once again, she purposely pulled savagely at my chains, but this time I was ready and swiped her legs right out from under her big round behind.

"Whoooaaa!" shouted a fellow guard.

"She got you pegged, Roste! Now we know who wears the pants!" Laughter echoed against the walls of the institution. Roste's face filled with rage. I sat quietly with a small smile across my face. It took Roste a few tries, but she was back up on her short pudgy legs.

"I'll show you a thing or two," she hissed through her crooked yellow teeth. But before she could bring down her righteous wrath, a stern loud voice rang out above the hoots and hollers.

"Let's get back to work, ladies. This is a correctional facility, not a wrestling ring!" The thin middle-aged woman stood tall with authority. Her washed out bleached blond hair fell loosely upon her broad shoulders while her small pointy nose offset her squared chin. But it was her deep blue eyes that immediately caught my attention.

"Roste, how many times do I have to tell you about physically assaulting new prisoners?" The warden shook her head with disgust.

"One more episode like this, Roste, and I'll have you transferred out of Five Miles. Do I make myself perfectly clear?" Roste snarled then hung her head low.

"Yes, Warden Shoole." Roste reluctantly moved away from me.

"My name is Warden Karen Shoole. Welcome to Five Miles Correctional Facility and your new home. I tolerate very little from prisoners and from the staff. You'll come to know I am very equal when disciplining those on both sides of the bars. Roste, you will see the prisoner safely to her cell." Warden Shoole turned on her heels and left us alone.

"This way," said Roste through gritted crooked teeth. As I walked shackled down the main corridor of the prison, shouts of obscenities and propositions rebounded against the cold cement walls.

"Here's your cell, Becker." Roste used a key to let me inside. This time, though, her push was more like just a friendly shove. She mumbled a few other undecipherable words as she unlocked my cuffs and shackles.

"Your cell mate is Madeline the Masher." Roste's grin was frightening. As she locked the heavy metal door, she gave me the finger. The cell was small with two flat bunk beds flush against the unpainted wall. A small chrome toilet sat along side the cracked porcelain sink in the far corner.

My roommate was far from cordial; not that I expected her to be anything less. Most convicted criminals hold on to a bit of the outside world by taking control of their surroundings in prison. I listened as she preached her rules of "do's and don'ts" and nodded in agreement every so often to let her know she was in charge. I rubbed at my raw wrists and black-and-blue ankles. The evening went by slow with little conversation from my prison buddy. Her name, Madeline the Masher, was more than understandable. Her short black hair cropped to the sides of her age filled face flaunted the fact she was definitely not a social butterfly. A large scar hauntingly peaked through her right cheek while a dark green bandana wrapped itself about her forehead then tied behind in a knot. But it was her six-foot muscular build and overdeveloped biceps that set her name in motion.

I was told by the Masher that chow at Five Miles facility was served normally during the early evening hours and that today would be no different just because an inmate was found dead in her cell. As I stood patiently waiting in line for my turn, I realized my appetite was slowly emerging as my stomach began to grumble from hunger pains. Slabs of ominous food were dumped upon my tray whether I wanted to try my luck or not. Even though I was quite hungry, the array of colorful grub did not appeal to me at all.

"Hey Bay!" howled an unfamiliar voice from behind. As I turned to look, I noticed a small group of women forming a half circle around me.

"You must be new here, sweetie. We're the welcoming party!" A tall heavy set brunette wearing a ponytail and an Ohio State baseball cap greedily took the liberty of placing her large hand on my shoulder. Exhaling a huge sigh and bearing just about enough from groping prison guards, I maneuvered myself around to grab her wrist disabling her as she yelped loudly in agonizing pain.

"Hey homie! I was just trying to be friendly not freaky! I'm into dicks, not pussy!" The frightened woman squirmed as I exerted more pressure on her overextended wrist. A couple of the other inmates stepped back and smiled at the confrontation. No one came to her defense.

"I don't like to be touched unless I want to be handled! Do we have an understanding here?" By now the guard was coming over to see who was causing the commotion.

"You're into trouble already?" asked a large African American woman. She pulled out her nightstick ready to use. I immediately released my grip on the other prisoner.

"Chill, sister! She don't mean no harm to me. We just gettin' to know each other, that's all up front." The ponytail prisoner remained calm and brushed herself off as if she were dirty. The correction officer eyed us both suspiciously.

"Go finish eating or I'll take you two back to your cells with empty stomachs!" threatened the dark skinned guard. I moved away from her and sat down alone at the far end of an empty table.

"Mandie, Mandie Haraloski is my name and hustling is my game!" Her crooked grin shined the most perfect white teeth I had ever seen. Without an invitation, Mandie's followers helped themselves to the empty seats across from me.

"Alix Becker." With my hand outstretched, I waited patiently for her response. She hesitantly looked me up and then down. Her grip surprisingly was light. Her smooth lineless face led me to believe she was relatively quite young.

"Ladies, introductions now!" commanded Mandie.

"Rhiana, Donnie, Jess, Adrian, Robbie, Mary Beth, Megan, and Linda." One by one each woman announced a name with a nod.

"I didn't mean to come on strong, Alix. It's just that we, I mean the girls and I, wanted to get to you before the wrong group of preemies knocked on your door. We may be criminals, but in here, we're the better of the lot. We won't kill you for a pack of cigarettes. Some of these women, well, you just don't want to get them mad," reported Mandie.

"So, Mandie. How do you know what type of prisoner I am?" I asked with extreme curiosity. Mandie flashed her gleaming teeth while the other girls chuckled.

"Shoot, Alix, you stand out like a virgin pussy!" Laughter filled the table. I had to smile at her natural spirit. If you would bypass and ignore the steel bars and the matching bright orange jumpsuits, it wouldn't be too hard to picture this group of women getting together at a neighborhood bar on Friday night after a long hard week of honest work.

Mandie kept the conversation going and the laughter intensified as I became a little bit more relaxed with this cloister of women prisoners. I listened with intent and made mental notes as Mandie explained how to get about within Five Miles.

"So Alix, how much time you got?" Mandie asked breaking my concentration.

"Time?" I asked quizzically.

"Yeah, how much time you in for?" asked Robbie, a short blond with big dimples. Her cheery face struck me as odd. Wire rimmed glasses sat crooked on her pudgy face. It looked as if her nose had been broken, more than once. An enormous lump erupted from the bridge between her flaring nostrils.

"Life." Silence filled the immediate area while all eyes were drawn to me.

"What ya' do?" Megan seemed reluctant to ask. I decided to leave out the fact I was a former FBI agent. I didn't think it would go over too well. For a moment I did not speak.

"It's okay, if you don't want to…" I cut Mandie off in mid-stream.

"I shoved a knife up through a woman's throat until it sliced into her brain killing her instantly." Mandies' eyes shot wide open while a couple of the other girls backed immediately away.

"She must have been some kind of witch hunter and deserved to be permanently cut!" Heads were nodding in unison as Mandie justified my crime.

"Well, the courts disagreed with you on that specific point," I retorted.

"Okay, ladies, let's move it out! Back to your cells on the double!" shouted one of the attending guards. The cafeteria erupted with groans and grumbles as hundreds of women lined up to go back to their jail bound bunks. Madeline the Masher was already in the cell when I arrived. She was reading a beat-up copy of the Old Testament. The binding of the paperback book had been split and ripped pages stuck out everywhere.

"The Lord will save you, if you let Him into your heart! Repent and be free," she announced as I sat down heavily on the bottom bunk. There on my flat pillow lay a small hand made wooden cross.

"This from you?" I asked.

"Well, it's not from the damn tooth fairy, you idiot! The Lord loves you so repent!"

Madeline stretched out and hummed some unknown melody. The large metal barred doors shut and locked with a loud clang. I closed my weary eyes and immediately my thoughts were consumed by Sierra's lovely image. Maybe some day she would find it in her heart to forgive me and the mess I had made of our lives. Once again, I fought so desperately to keep inside the building emotions I so eagerly wanted to release.

I must have dozed as the night grew near when suddenly I was awakened by an intruding bright light shining directly into my face. A familiar creepy chuckle echoed inside the chilly cell.

"Thought I'd forget about my new baby?" Roste's sweaty and smelly body permeated the entire area.

"I told you I'd come back! I'm so horny!" Roste reached in and pulled me out by the hair. Excruciating pain seared down my head into my back.

"The Lord will save you if you let Him into your heart!" Madeline the Masher was preaching her words as Roste was about to have her way with me. Unfortunately, I knew I would be punished if I should take the risk and resist her womanly assault.

"Stay out of this Masher, it doesn't involve you. She's mine!" Roste shut off the flashlight before she ripped savagely at my orange suit. My decision was spontaneous. I couldn't stop myself as I forcefully pushed her away and physically refused her obvious delusions of unwarranted affection.

"I said, repent! Repent for your sins! The Lord will forgive you!" With that a quick "whoosh" flew above my head. Roste stumbled backwards and hit hard against the steel bars. Madeline the Masher had jumped down and stood face to face with Lauren Roste.

"I told you Masher to mind your manners, this doesn't involve you!" But Madeline would not move. Instead, with full force behind her large body she swung a small rounded club directly into Roste's protruding belly.

"Repent your sins!" she cried as Roste yelled out in pain. Within seconds Roste crumpled to the floor as Madeline immediately snatched the keys which hung loosely from her waist. It took only a split second to unlock and open the door.

"Now go and repent your sins." Cautiously Madeline dragged the crying Roste into the cold dark hallway then tossed out the keys after relocking the cell. Roste cradled her stomach as she groaned in agony. Finally, after a few minutes of writhing on the ground, Roste seemed to crawl away and disappear. I was taken back and grateful for Madeline's intervention.

"Madeline, I appreciate what you did for me." Madeline pushed me aside as she heaved herself back up onto the top bunk.

"As I said before, ask forgiveness and He shall forgive your sins! Repent, this is the word!" She hummed a few notes and settled herself down. Within minutes, it was quiet once again. This time I welcomed the solitude of darkness that engulfed the solace of my meager surroundings.

The remainder of the night passed away without incident, but I could no longer sleep after my unannounced and intruding visit from Roste. The prison cells were damp and cold and the old thin blanket given to each inmate provided little warmth. It was hard to believe that just a short time ago, I was dreaming of my new life with Sierra in the warmth of my own sweet home. And now, within a snap of a finger, I was sentenced to live out the remainder of my days sharing a dismal cell with a harden criminal.

In lei of it all, I could not help but to remain grateful to Madeline for saving my dignity and the physical trauma that Roste intended to inflict on my tired and drained body. Word must have spread around for when it came to showers, no one even bothered to look my way. This, to me, was a blessing in disguise.

As for Mandie's unending determination to mold me into "one of her girls" it became quite inspiring. With her extended prison connections, she made sure that my reputation reflected that of a ruthless and heartless killer. It sealed the door on confrontations and left, without a doubt, no room for discussion or disagreement. But as time granted a distorted perception of serenity, the days and nights meshed and blended into one another, making it unusually difficult to place a day with a date deep within the hallow prison walls.

In order to keep a fine line of measured sanity, I began to listen and take an interest in each of the stories told by Mandie's circle of comrades. It was amazing to hear their tales of woe as few of them would not see the outside of the prison walls for at least 20 years, if not more. As it stood, Mandie faced a maximum of 30 years for her part in a grand theft auto brigade. Sadly enough, it had been her first offense, and I too, thought the punishment was a bit extreme. But as she told me detailed information about her trial, I realized an uncanny connection had surfaced. This anomaly went by the name of Judge Patrick McHenry! I urgently passed this important information on to Maria in dire desperation. I remembered how Sherrie was so adamant about the dishonesty and foul play conducted by McHenry. Sherrie had sworn up and down about his itchy fingers and the large sums of cash that had passed undetected straight into his private account. He was indeed, an unscrupulous and deceitful man.

I had always been a true believer in the ideals of the American judicial system. But now, with just a few months under my belt living on the inside of the barbwire fence, I could understand how apprehension and mental instability crept inside each and every day searching to extinguish the burning flame called hope.

As I lay awake within the grips of iron bars, I tried so desperately to hold on to myself and the wonderful memories of Sierra in a world where only we exist. I envisioned how our lives would have been, if only we could be freed from our unconscionable predestined fate. But as the reiteration of slamming metal doors echoed within the prison of solidarity, the grim reality of it all sucked me back in. Once again, I quietly cried myself, as I had done so many other lonely nights, into yet another unsettled sleep.

CHAPTER 18

Days, weeks then months at Five Miles rushed together as I served my time and grew closer to Mandie and her associates. The weather outside grew warmer with the upcoming change in season. It was on one of the spring like days Mandie suggested our first outdoor team game.

"What say we strike up a volley ball match on the courts this morning?" asked Mandie with a crooked smile. I couldn't help but to ponder, what her life must have been like before she made that one regretful mistake. Her calming blue eyes and rosy cheeks gave little impression of the desperation and anxiety felt by that of a single mother of three. What drives a person to risk their entire way of life for the sheer existence of striving to obtain the unreachable?

"So what do you say, Alix; are you up for a little balling?" She lightly nudged my ribs with her pointed elbow.

"Gotta keep fit in here, you know, or your muscles will turn to jelly. Hey girls, up for some ball tossing?" Mandie opened the invitation. Most of the women at the surrounding tables nodded in agreement.

"Sure, why not!" I responded without delay.

Within a matter of minutes, a good portion of the women from Cell Block D and E were outside in the prison yard. Many began pumping iron with the weight equipment that sat against the north wall. Some of the more athletic types were already in deep concentration playing basketball. Mandie and the girls flagged down the sand enclosed area designed specifically for the game of volleyball.

"Mandie, I never asked you this before, but do you know why they call this place Five Miles?" I asked quizzically.

"That's simple, sweetheart. It's called Five Miles because the nearest sign of life isn't for at least five miles in any direction from this hell hole! So if you're planning on an escape route, you better steal a truck or you've got a long hefty walk to the nearest town. I don't know of anyone who had actually made it to the outside, if you know what I mean." She winked at me then tossed the ball over the net.

"Looking to fly the coop already?" questioned Mandie with a flashy grin that exposed her perfect set of white teeth. For a brief moment, the thought was more than tempting.

"Play ball!" commanded Mandie. She threw the ball straight up in the air and with her large hand hit it hard. The volleyball flew rapidly with precision just missing the top of the net. A dark Asian woman jumped up and tried desperately to return the powerful serve. She completely missed falling wildly into the net.

"You're nothing but a fat ass cheater!" she cried out at Mandie.

"That was a perfectly good serve! Don't blame me because you can't move that lazy Asian carcass of yours! Give the ball back, it's still our serve!" Mandie moved urgently from the back of the court and headed toward the middle of the net. The Asian woman angered by Mandie's verbal abuse moved swiftly to meet her opponent. The game hadn't even been in play five minutes and already a fight was in the making. I stood to the side and observed the two women as they went at each other like cats and dogs. Mandie threw the first connecting right hook, only for the Asian woman to return with a solid left. As the two women brawled and thrashed about both tower guards stood watching as if enjoying the prison yard commotion. Within moments of the fight breaking out, a large crowd had gathered about the two swinging fisted women.

Suddenly, without warning, loud above the shouts and jeers of the other prisoners, a single shot echoed high over our heads between the cement walls. There stood tall and mighty the attractive and well versed Warden Karen Shoole. Her loaded shot gun rested evenly on her muscular thigh.

"That's enough, ladies! If you all can't get along and play nice, then you won't play at all! Is that understood?" she bellowed. The gathered body of convicts became silent.

"Good, I'm glad all of you understand because you just forfeited the remainder of time you had left outside. Guards, move them all in, now!" she commanded. Instantly, several women correctional officers began to herd the convicts together and ushered the lot back to each of their designated cells. As we were marched inside, I noticed Mandie's eye had begun to swell and I knew from experience it would eventually turn out to be a painful black eye.

"You have a visitor, Becker, come with me." One of the husky guards grabbed my arm and pulled as I was about to enter my cell. I walked in silence to a holding room and there to greet me was Maria and Sherrie. I was filled with hope at their glimmering and most welcomed faces.

"Are you here to get me out?" I asked praying for the answer I've longed for since my arrival here at Five Miles. But sadly enough, as fast as their smiles appeared, they vanished. Filled with disappointment and despair, I sat heavily down onto the small metal chair placed directly across from them.

"How are they treating you, Alix?" asked Maria with reservation.

"Well, I have the penthouse in Cell Block D area that comes with a wonderful view of the ocean! And the room service here, oh, how do I describe it, well, it's just to die for!" I responded sarcastically. The hurt in Maria's saddened eyes was unbearable. I felt horrible and irritated by my lack of sensitivity. Sherrie remained quiet.

"I'm so sorry, Maria. I didn't mean..." Maria stopped me in mid-sentence.

"It's alright, Alix. I failed you as your attorney, and...as your friend. I don't blame you for your pessimistic attitude. I would feel the same if I were in your shoes." Her lovely brown eyes filled with tears.

"No, you, of all people, don't deserve my wrath! Please forgive my stupidity!" I immediately got up to give Maria a hug when suddenly the cell door flew open and the guard came bouncing in.

"Sit your ass down, Becker!" But before I could protest, the wheeling guard swung violently using her night stick with a direct hit into the middle of my back. Immense pain seared up through my spine sending me straight down onto my knees to the floor.

"Stop this unwarranted assault!" screamed Maria as she bent down to help me. Sherrie was already on the floor trying to ease me up.

"What is wrong with you?" The guard stood above sneering down at all three of us.

"I thought she was going to get physical with you, Ms. Shiner. We're responsible for the prisoners here at Five Miles." She snapped her gum and turned to leave. The pain in my back slowly began to subside.

"Alix, we're here because we have an appeal date in court. I was able to call in a few favors and move your date up to early next week. We will come back for you. I'm not through, Alix. I promise I *will* get you out!" Maria pulled me close. I staggered a bit trying to regain my composure.

"Sierra?" My words were short and few. Maria moved slightly away then glanced at Sherrie.

"Alix, I don't know how to break the news to you…" Maria turned away as Sherrie stepped forward.

"She's…gone, Alix." Sherrie bit at her trembling lower lip. All at once, my entire world crumpled down around me. It didn't matter anymore if I ever left this horrendous place of hell. My embittered spirit wracked aimlessly at my disheartened body while tiny specks of tears flittered upon my flushed cheeks.

"Times up, let's go!" interrupted the abusive guard.

"Alix, please hold on!" begged Sherrie.

"We'll be back next week to escort you to the appeal hearing," she murmured. Maria, with her head down, remained quiet. Then, without warning, the brooding guard roughly grabbed me by my elbow to shackle me once again. Within seconds, she was eagerly shoving me down the corridor back to my cell. Madeline the Masher was busily humming her prayers.

"You'll *never* leave this place alive!" taunted the angry guard as she locked the metal bars in place. I walked robotically to my uncomfortable bunk. Instinctively, I curled up inside myself trying to block out the inevitable.

"You know, if you believe, your sins will be forgiven and you shall find salvation," chanted Madeline. I eagerly squeezed my eyes shut while hoarding back the overwhelming abundance of mixed feelings that surged throughout my exhausted body. Madeline and her preaching merged as one and became just words with no meaning.

After the shocking and devastating news of Sierra's death, I stayed to myself not wanting to deal with the dramas of prison life. Mandie kept on me until I finally told her about the unbearable and unspeakable catastrophe.

"Even though I'm into dick, I can dig where you're coming from, Alix. Sometimes I think about how much I miss my kids…and…well, anyways, it's never easy losing someone you love, girl. I'm here if you need me." Mandie gave me a slight hug and left me alone. Then with utter respect for my privacy, she signaled to the others so that I was given plenty of personal space. My grieving for Sierra would cling to me as long as I lived deep inside within these prison walls.

As the upcoming appeal drew near, the emptiness which consumed my inner spirit remained as a constant reminder of my ever lasting love for Sierra. Maria and Sherrie had manipulated the system a bit and were given special permission to travel with me to the courthouse. Warden Shoole resisted this unusual request until Maria had little choice but to present the official court order for passage. Reluctantly, Warden Shoole agreed, but only if a prison guard accompanied me at all times. And of course, I must remain handcuffed and shackled during the entire route to and from the hearing.

Much to my surprise, as we left the perimeters of the prison, the media had been waiting patiently to get a quick photograph for their ruthless tabloids. Camera crews and trucks were lined up on both sides of the roadway.

"What's this?" I asked quizzically. Maria and Sherrie sat on the bench located on the opposite side. They, too, peered through barred windows at the wild show.

"We didn't want you to get your hopes up, but your case headlined every major newspaper across the country. There were even peaceful demonstrations in front of the White House in honor of your defense. You hit a nerve, Alix! There have been hundreds and hundreds of phone calls and emails delivered to the President insisting you should be set free!" proudly announced Sherrie. The van haphazardly moved around the shouting reporters then immediately picked up speed.

"Oh, for heaven's sakes, where did you learn how to drive?" Maria tried to pound on the metal cage. Once again, the van swerved but this time we all took a tumble in the back of the paddy wagon. Sherrie hurriedly shot forward across the seat. Within an instant, she violently slammed her head against the back of the cab.

"My head!" Sherrie cried out in pain. Maria was beyond furious.

"Hey asshole, slow down!" Once again, Maria tried frantically to bang on the connecting piece. The police vehicle escalated even faster as the reckless driver maneuvered it with no regards for the occupants inside. Suddenly, without any warning, the driver swerved off the marked highway onto a grassy dirt road that dead ended into a realm of thick protective trees.

"What is wrong with this woman and where are we?" shouted Sherrie as she so desperately tried to gain her balance. Immediately, my self-pity eluded me as I instantly realized that my dear and close friends were in grave danger.

"Wouldn't *you* like to know," cackled the correction officer. My mind swiftly switched gears and I recognized right away the gruff familiar voice. It was none other than Roste and she was laughing hysterically like a mad woman!

"Roste! These women are attorneys; you can't play them, Roste! Roste! Do you hear me?" I shouted through the wire barrier.

Sherrie held a tissue to her slight wound. Maria was busily checking Sherrie to make sure she didn't sustain any other cuts or bruises. Within moments of stopping, the back doors flew open wide. Roste stood perfectly still as she aimed the loaded shot gun directly at Maria's chest.

"You got an awful big mouth, attorney friend. And I'm about to shut you up!" Roste cocked back the trigger.

"No, Roste!" I yelled as I quickly moved in front of Maria.

"You'll wind up behind bars with me for killing an unarmed attorney. Then all of your playmates back at Five Miles will be *playing* you! Is that what you really want, Roste?" Panic seized me as I watched her take aim disregarding my stern warning.

"Think about it Roste! Is that what you really want?" Reluctantly, Roste lowered her weapon then spat on the ground.

"Nope, I guess not. My daddy be real mad at me…I want to stay outside the bars." She tilted her head and tried to smile as her front buck teeth poked out. Maria and Sherrie were in shock by the ruthlessness of Lauren Roste.

"Get out of the van, attorney friends, I want to have a good look at you." She sniffed then snorted. Maria quickly glanced my way for approval.

"Didn't you hear me; get the hell out of the van?" Once again, Roste swung up the heavy firearm and this time aimed it at Sherrie's head.

"Okay, okay, I'm getting out right now." Maria was visibly shaken by this traumatic ordeal. I, on the other hand, was busily trying to figure a way out of this dangerous situation.

"You touch me, you redneck hillbilly and…" But before Maria could finish her over zealous threat, Roste instantly swung the butt of the rifle into Maria's unprotected face.

"Aaaaagh!" yelped Maria as she desperately cupped the blood which spewed profoundly from her busted nose. Sherrie screamed and instinctively dived down to aid her wailing partner.

"Roste! What is wrong with you?" I shouted from inside the van. The area was deserted and Roste knew she was the one in control.

"Shut up! I got suspended with no pay for three days cause of you! Get out now agent lady!" I shimmed myself out and slid down onto the grassy ground.

"Now, I'm gonna do what I should have done to you the first time." She licked her dry cracked lips. With the gun lowered, she yanked at my prison garb ripping the buttons off the orange shirt.

"You got nice titties," she drooled. In the meantime, Sherrie used her jacket and gently held it to Maria's face. Maria moaned in agony through the stained garment.

"McHenry isn't going to like this one bit," I spouted. Suddenly, Roste remained still. Her crooked grin disappeared at the mention of the judge's name. It was a long shot and I took it with leaps and bounds.

"He don't have to know what happened here," she mumbled. Bingo! I got her! For a moment, I tried to ingest her reluctant response.

"How will he *not* find out? You may be able to hide this from Warden Shoole but not Judge Patrick McHenry!" I pushed her buttons even more.

"He said I could do whatever I want, just don't get caught," she wined. A light trail of spittle slowly dripped from her protruding lip.

"Come on, Roste. You're smarter than that! He said do what you want because *you* will be the one that gets caught and then he doesn't have to deal with your sorry ass any longer." I shrugged my shoulders. You could see the wheels turning as Roste became furious.

"Why that two timing, no good, weasel of a judge? All the money he gives me is not enough to go to prison for the rest of my life! I got stuff on him and I bet the newspapers would pay a bundle..." Roste was thinking now.

"You're smarter than you look, Roste. It's about time you get what you truly deserve. You're going to let a *man* tell you what to do? I find that very hard to believe." I turned and looked over at Maria and Sherrie. Maria was lying flat on the ground and had passed out from the extreme pain of her injury, or so I thought. Sherrie dared not say a word.

"Did you know McHenry does dyke women?" Roste chuckled. For a moment, I was amazed by her unannounced forthcoming.

"I hear he did Lena Harris." I decided to throw out her name as bait to see if I could catch something just a little bit more than Roste was willing to give.

"Hell, he did her more than once. In fact, she did anybody and everybody! She was nothin' more than a White House whore!" Roste slapped her thigh and snorted like a pig.

"I bet McHenry liked to play 'head dick' with Lena's friends at the Taylor Mansion too, eh?" I thought I might as well give it all or nothing.

"I'd never seen anything like it before." Roste seemed to be mesmerized by the sexual flashbacks.

"All those bodies in leather, women on women and then McHenry walks right in and he does each of them, one by one. What a sight!" Sherrie and I listened with disgust.

"You were there?" I questioned with doubt.

"Well, hell, why not? McHenry liked to have extra security when he was around so I volunteered for the job. Got to see it all and sometimes got a piece for myself. Know what I'm talkin' about?" She hastily grabbed at my breast. I stood my ground while this nasty woman man handled me.

"I'm aiming to do the same to you!" Roste released me then shifted the heavy weapon.

"Why don't you just ask for it, Lauren?" Roste's beady eyes grew wide as her sheepish grin disappeared.

"No one calls me by my God given name! No one except my mama!" Roste swung the awkward firearm into position then took aim. My heart began to beat wildly at the horrible thought of being shot. Within that split second she cocked the hammer, Sherrie lunged fearlessly upward knocking Roste off her feet and sending the bullet harmlessly somewhere out into the woods.

"You're gonna' be sorry," cried Roste as she struggled to get up. By this time, I had straddled her wide body with mine and begun to pound her face with my cuffed hands.

"Alix, stop!" shouted Sherrie while frantically pulling me back. Roste's bloodied face was unrecognizable as she lay unconscious by my vicious lethal blows.

"Is she dead?" Sherrie asked in almost a whisper. With shaky legs, I awkwardly stood up then delved deep inside her pockets to search for the key to set me free.

"No, she's not dead; just taking a nice long nap," I retorted while reclaiming the small silver key.

"It feels good to get these off!" I said with relief. The cuffs snapped open and fell to the ground.

"Thank you, Sherrie, for saving my life." Sherrie instantly blushed with embarrassment.

"Hey, what about me?" mumbled Maria. Her nose was twice the size as it should be.

"I hope you hit her extra hard for me!" Maria's words were muffled but I knew exactly what she said.

"What did you think of Roste's confession? Can we use it?" I asked hoping to hear the right answer.

"I got it all," murmured Maria. With her red stained hand, she held up her small cell phone. I nodded my head in astonishment then smiled.

"Besides, we should have enough evidence now to go back and slam dunk McHenry!" stated Sherrie.

"The media will smear his fine and upstanding reputation across the front pages of every tabloid and local newspaper in this city!" Sherrie was delighted with his upcoming downfall.

"We now have our connection between Harris and McHenry. And I bet if we dig deep enough, we'll find out about the other dirty connections he made during his tenure as judge." We nodded in agreement. I knew McHenry wasn't about to lie down and play dead. He would fight us to the bitter end; but with a lot of hard work and support from Maria's political contacts, we might stand a fighting chance.

"What are you going to do with sleeping beauty?" asked Maria. Dark rings were beginning to form under her droopy eyes.

"I'm going to cuff her and we can take her back with us to the courthouse. I guess I missed my appeal hearing." We all began to laugh at the injustice of it all.

Maria had ignored Sherrie's insistent plea for a quick stop by the hospital emergency room. We arrived at the courthouse within the hour. Roste remained unconscious and secured in the back end of the police van. Maria couriered a sealed note to Judge Patrick McHenry. I was sure by now the police van had been reported missing since we were considerably late for the hearing. Within minutes, McHenry demanded a formal meeting in his chambers. At Maria's suggestion, I changed into my street clothes which Maria had brought for my appeal.

As we sat in silence in the elaborate high back cushioned chairs, I glanced about the room at the hundreds of volumes of law books that were arranged meticulously amongst the deep red oak shelves. For a brief second, my keen sense of apprehension kicked in and I felt slightly unsettled as if something was about to go terribly wrong. And before I could voice my concerns to Maria and Sherrie, two armed security guards burst their way inside the enormous wooden chamber doors holding their guns high.

"What is the meaning of this?" yelled Maria.

"Sit down and shut up!" the armed man shouted back.

"Alixandria Becker! We have a warrant for your arrest! Come with us!" demanded the shorter of the two men.

"Just a minute, you have no right to take Alix anywhere! We're here at the request of Judge Patrick McHenry! Now I advise you two to turn around and just trot yourselves out the door!" Sherrie looked terrified as Maria took a stand against the gun toting adversaries. The uniformed imposters snickered by Maria's demands and her swollen face.

"You got a really big mouth for an attorney, maybe that's why your nose is broken; someone tried to shut you up!" The boisterous men burst out laughing and edged in closer. Maria was not afraid and took a step forward. Impulsively, I grabbed her arm and held her back. The taller of the two lunged out at Maria shoving her backward into the chair.

"He didn't tell us these loudmouths would be so much trouble! We should get paid double for this!" The nasty man's eyes narrowed. A sadistic smirk slowly formed across his contorted face. With his weapon steady and outstretched in front of him, he began to unbuckle his pants.

"Hey, Ron, ever do it to a dyke?" The two men inched in a bit closer. By now, Sherrie had retreated back behind me while Maria quickly got up from her sitting position.

"Nope, Johnny, but I heard…" His voice was cut short.

"You pigs!" shouted Sherrie filled with fear. Instinctively, they both cackled by her child like actions. Johnny, the taller of the two men, eyed Maria while holding his crotch with his free hand.

"It's waiting for *you*, sweetheart! Come and get it!" With that, Johnny cautiously laid his weapon on the small round table.

"Cover me, Ron. I want to show this little lady attorney what a real man can do!" Ron held his gun up while Johnny continued to unzip his trousers.

"I like to watch, Johnny, but then I want a turn!" He gestured toward Sherrie. It was within that split second of distraction and before they could pat themselves on the back for a job well done, I lunged forward, catching Ron off guard and by surprise. As Johnny hurriedly tried to pull his pants back together, I expertly disarmed Rob of his weapon and roughly yanked at his delicate manhood. As he lay howling in agony from the excruciating blow to his genitals, Johnny made a desperate attempt to try and remedy the situation. Regretfully, the gun when off and Johnny staggered a bit then dropped to the floor. The open wound in his shoulder oozed a bright red liquid.

"Sorry about that Johnny. Since you were in such a hurry to give Maria what you got, maybe I should just go ahead and take it anyway!" I aimed the gun directly between his legs.

"No! No! Please don't shoot me there!" he whimpered in pain. Immediately, Maria retrieved the other hand gun.

"You're gonna' be sorry," whispered Ron as he rolled to and fro on the floor. Within a flash, Maria held the gun steady against the side of Ron's temple.

"Go ahead, asshole! Give me a reason to blow your head off!" Maria had a firm hold on herself and remained completely unshaken.

"Okay, okay, we were never gonna hurt you. We were just gonna' have a little fun, that's all," blurted Ron.

"Right Johnny?" But Johnny could only whine from the increasing pain emanating from the gaping hole within his shoulder.

"Johnny?" Ron nervously called out.

"As you already know, Ron, I have been convicted of murder and sentenced to life in prison without parole. So it doesn't make any difference to me if I kill you or your friend. Understand?" Ron nervously shook his head.

"Who hired you to mess with us?" asked Maria while pushing the gun against the back of Ron's head. For a moment, Ron remained silent.

"You don't get it, we're dead men if we tell," he whispered trembling by this unexpected trauma.

"*You* don't get it! You're dead men if you *don't* tell!" Maria roughly shoved the gun into the side of his temple.

"Maria, you're beginning to scare me. I think you might be enjoying this!" commented Sherrie under her breath.

"Okay, okay, I'll tell you everything, just don't...don't kill me," he begged as sweat poured off his face. It was that Judge McHenry guy who hired us. His orders were to "take care" of you permanently without repercussions and tie up any loose ends. I swear it's the truth!" Ron curled into a tight ball of fear. We knew now McHenry never had any intention of meeting with Maria or any of us, for that matter. It was a ruse to get us inside his chambers where the only way we could possibly leave would be in a body bag. I should have known McHenry would never hold true to his word. He was more than just a dirty judge; he was downright deadly. By hiring these criminals he had become an accessory to attempted murder. For sure, Maria and Sherrie would be able to seal the lid on McHenry's coffin. The search for Patrick McHenry was on. For Maria and Sherrie it was just the beginning.

Within the next few days, a search warrant was issued and all of McHenry's papers and electronic files were confiscated as evidence. His expensive home in Arlington was searched from top to bottom where hidden discs were discovered revealing highly unusual and compromising positions which involved himself and the late Lena Harris.

It didn't take long before the media got wind of the story and the infamous name of Lena Harris, once a prestigious member on the White House staff, now suddenly became discredited with her affiliation to the President.

As for the ongoing investigation of the mysterious murders, it had been quickly seized from the jurisdiction of the FBI and buried deep within an ominous governmental team centered in the heart of Washington D.C.

In lieu of all that had transpired since my trial and incarceration, the murder charge against me had been conveniently dropped. I was to be reinstated with honors and given the official title of Special Agent for the FBI. I refused, much to everyone's surprise, both position and title without any bonding reservations.

"Maria, I can't help but think about Mandie and her prisoner buddies. They, too, had been trapped inside the echo of lies." Maria and Sherrie smiled.

"We already have our associates working on each one of their individual cases as we speak. They're in good hands, now Alix. Thanks to you!" explained Sherrie.

"Alix, since technically you're out of a job, would you mind helping us out?" questioned Maria. Sherrie looked away as I eyed both of them suspiciously.

"We need to find Patrick McHenry. It seems he was picked up only to be released two hours later on a bond of an undisclosed amount. Anyway, he high tailed it out of the country. My informants say he's hiding somewhere in Mexico." I sat down next to her desk.

"So now you want me to be your bounty hunter?" I asked playfully.

"What's wrong with being a bounty hunter?" replied Sherrie while shrugging her shoulders.

"We've got a problem though, I don't speak any Spanish." Maria shook her finger at my resistance.

"I arranged for a friend of yours to help you out," responded Maria. She was searching for something on her desk.

"She's the best computer hacker in the country and she has an unofficial contract with the government," boasted Maria.

"Her name is Bette Craigen." Maria stood up to leave. She then handed me an envelope containing an airline ticket and a wad of cash.

"Wait a minute! I haven't seen Bette in almost..." Maria cut me off midstream.

"Yes, and she can hardly wait to see you! Now, hurry up because you're going to miss your flight." Before either one of them could make another move, I purposely blocked the exit forcing them to confront and listen to me.

"What do you want me to do if I find him?" I asked quizzically as my heart skipped a beat.

"Well, bring our friend home, of course." Maria gently pushed me aside.

CHAPTER 19

My early flight into Mexico City turned out to be rough and bumpy. The skies hung low and were filled with rain and humidity as I scurried down the steps of the small turbine plane. The cramped terminal was filled with American tourists. I looked around in hopes of spotting my friend Bette. Much to my surprise, I didn't see her anywhere. I decided to follow the crowd to the baggage area. There I waited anxiously to retrieve my black bag filled with the basic necessities.

"Buenos diás!" exclaimed a young dark skinned man.

"El taxi?" he asked. I remained silent for a moment since I did not speak a single word of Spanish.

"Creo que no" responded a woman from behind. I automatically turned around and there standing close was my good friend, Bette Craigen. Within a split second he accepted the rejection and moved on to the next out-of-towner. Suddenly, and much to my delight, we both became entangled in each other's arms. As we slowly separated, I realized it had been almost eight years since I had seen her round and happy face.

"Alix, it's so good to see you again after all these years!" she stated gleefully. Her short pudgy stature was how I remembered her best. Her skin was brown from the tanning sun and her light brown hair glistened under the strained fluorescent airport lights. Her clothes were loosely fit with an over abundant amount of flowery colors.

"I've missed you, Bette." My heart was sincere while my eyes brimmed with tears of joy. Her warm embrace was spontaneous and quite welcomed.

"I know you've been through a tremendous ordeal, Alix. I'm so sorry to hear about Sierra." At the mention of her name, I suddenly broke down in the middle of the small airport. With a supporting arm about my waist, Bette gently escorted me outside to our transportation.

"I didn't mean to lose it back there," I sobbed. Bette nodded and remained silent.

"It's alright, Alix, you take your time," comforted Bette. I dabbed my eyes and quickly tried to compose myself.

"You've always been a good friend to me, Bette. I know over the years our personal contact has been minimal, but deep inside you hold a special place in my heart." I was feeling extremely sentimental and Bette was more than willing to be the recipient of my outreaching affection.

"Why don't we go grab a bite to eat," Bette softly suggested. I eagerly agreed with a half grin.

The long ride through the beautiful green countryside distracted me briefly from the grief I had been carrying since the death of Sierra. We bounced along the wayside road as we headed toward the motel located on the outskirts of town.

"Here we are!" announced Bette. She swung the compact car into the paved parking lot at the Calypso Restaurant. I was impressed by the elegance and style of this longstanding landmark.

"It's one of the finer places to dine in Sayulita. It's been remodeled by the Manuel brothers who trained as chefs in the fine-dining bistros and restaurants located in Los Angeles." Bette was pleased by her choice of dining milieu.

"It's very eloquent," I commented. Inside I was amazed at the beautifully polished wooden bar which must have stretched well over twenty feet in length.

"Dos!" Bette requested politely to the attending host. The tall attractive woman nodded with a smile and gestured for us to follow her into the exquisite dining area. Our round white covered table sat near a giant three-dimensional sculpture created by the notorious Ropi, a world renowned Mexican architect. The entire restaurant was filled with various Mexican antiques including famous artwork and surprisingly relics of Spanish household goods.

"Muchas Gracias" thanked Bette.

"Comer con gusto!" the pleasant woman responded.

"What did you say?" I asked with interest.

"Well, I first told her there were two of us, then I thanked her and she responded by telling us to enjoy our meal!" Bette was busily placing her silk napkin upon her lap. The menu was long and full of words I could not read

"I'm sorry, Alix. I know you can't speak nor read a word of Spanish. Let me help you. Did you want me to start at the top?" questioned Bette.

"I think it would be easier if I just tell you what I would like to eat," I responded. Within moments our server arrived and Bette placed the request for our meals. It wasn't long before we were eagerly eating our overabundant leafy salads.

"I'm sure Maria briefed you on the situation and what we will be up against," I commented. Bette sipped at her cold glass of ice water with squeezed lemon.

"I found him," she replied in between bites. For a moment I was stunned.

"McHenry, I know where he's hiding, Alix." Bette gave me a quick wink.

"This is delicious!" she boasted. I couldn't eat a thing and just stared in awe at my incredible friend.

"Oh, alright, I guess this can't wait until after we eat," replied Bette nonchalantly as she looked at my curious face.

"I tracked McHenry's account to a small Mexican bank here in Sayulita. He's been having large amounts of money transferred in from off shore accounts housed originally in Brazil and Siberia of all places. He's pretty slick!" Bette played with the leaves in her salad. Just then our main meal arrived and the delectable aroma stirred up my hunger pangs once again.

"Dig in!" she insisted with delight. Bette was right; the food was more than delicious! After a few minutes of delving into the flavorful Mexican cuisine, Bette stopped for a second to discuss the situation.

"Oh, and you know what's kind of strange? McHenry's been buying real estate in Greece. I think when he's ready to fly the coop he's got a place to stay, but that's just my opinion." She graciously wiped her tiny mouth.

"Where's he hiding out?" I asked with great interest.

"He's held up at one of the last haciendas right outside the city limits of Sayulita." She then took another huge bite of her bread and began to chew with vigor. My stomach felt full and suddenly I became very tired. Bette, too, sat back and relaxed.

"La cuenta, por favor?" Bette asked the server.

"Sí," the polite server responded instantly. I was highly impressed by Bette's extreme familiarity with the Spanish language and culture. As we left the restaurant, the storm clouds had cleared and the sun was shining brightly as the temperatures soared into the high 80's. Humidity hung heavy in the air and I immediately felt wet and sticky.

"I knew you wouldn't mind so I checked us in at the Puebla Inn. It's nothing fancy. I really didn't want to draw too much attention. We're supposed to be on vacation so we should act like tourists." Bette expertly swung the compact car out of the parking lot onto the main road. The inn was only a few minutes away. Once inside our room, we were able to discuss our plan of action.

"I took the liberty of checking out the area where he lives. He's got quite a setup. There are cameras everywhere supported by a high tech security system." Bette pulled out her slim line laptop and began to type away.

"Here, take a look for yourself," she said turning it around for me to see. There on the screen was a satellite view of his entire home and the surrounding land. She clicked a few buttons and suddenly it was if we were standing right above looking down on top of his roof. Once again, she maneuvered the view to various angles exposing several cameras mounted on the outside of the villa. Then, to make matters even worse, there loomed a six foot high brick wall surrounding the entire immediate grounds.

"Well, what do you think," she asked. I released a huge sigh at the thought of trying to break into his dwelling without getting caught and landing inside a dreadful Mexican prison.

"I don't know what to think," I replied honestly. Bette smiled and gave a slight chuckle.

"Does he live alone?" I questioned with curiosity.

"I've scoped out the perimeters and used heat sensors to comb the inside of the house. If anyone else is in there, I will know." Bette was studying the flat screen.

"McHenry's over confident, Alix. He buys the local police and he knows the US doesn't exactly get along with the Mexican government. So, he feels secure with cameras and high tech toys," she replied with confidence and reassurance.

"I can get you inside without a problem." Her fingers busily flew across the keyboard.

"I'll reroute the cameras on the outside and disarm the security alarm, if needed. Once you're inside, I'll freeze the surveillance videos so at least you don't have to worry about being seen. As for your persuasive techniques to encourage the judge himself to return to the US of A, well, the ball's in your court, old friend!" Bette sat back lazily in the wooden chair.

"Oh, I'll hook you up to a transmitter. This way we can stay in contact with one another and I can track where you are at all times. How's that for service?" asked Bette. I was truly impressed by Bette's knowledge and how she took the liberty of setting up the operation even before I arrived in Mexico. We discussed our plans in further detail.

"It would seem the judge likes to have his way with women and he pays handsomely for the company. Tomorrow night McHenry has arranged to have several prostitutes from the local whorehouse attend a private party. According to the agenda I extracted from his laptop, invitations were sent out to five local politicians." Bette sat quietly for a moment before a tiny grin inched across her adorable face.

"Wait a minute; I'm going in disguised as a hooker?" I exclaimed in disbelief.

"A prostituta!" she replied. Bette tried desperately to conceal her obvious amusement at the thought of me camouflaged as a woman of the night. Suddenly, we both burst out laughing.

"No, silly, you'll slip in at the same time McHenry's guests arrive," she responded sheepishly.

"Even though it would be a sight to see you dressed in black tights, high heels and a skimpy nightie!" she giggled with absolute delight.

"Very funny," I mumbled.

"McHenry will temporarily disarm his security system until his guests have arrived. The group of women will come all at once. I think this would be the best time for you to make your entrance. McHenry will be paying more attention to his next blow job rather than thinking about an intruder. Don't you think?" she commented casually. I silently nodded in agreement.

"How are you going to persuade him to leave Mexico, Alix?' Bette was busily setting up the vitals for tomorrow night's visit.

"I thought I might reason with him, and if that doesn't work, give him something so he can sleep on it." Bette knew exactly what I had in mind.

"I get it. Drag his sorry unconscious ass right out the front door. I personally know the pharmacist at the local drugstore in town. We'll pick up a wild cocktail tomorrow afternoon. But do you have a Plan B if by some chance you can't get him to cooperate?" asked Bette eagerly.

"Well, there's always the good ole' fashion way; by threatening to blow his head off!" I replied.

"So, I hope he doesn't put up too much of a fight and I don't have to worry about him yelling for help. Comprender?" I asked.

"Sí" she responded with a smile. After fine tuning the details on the abduction of Patrick McHenry, we decided to kick back and eagerly catch up on the years between us that had snuck up so quickly. After hours of chit-chatting about anything and everything, our minds grew tired and we both fell instantly asleep without even saying "Buenos noches."

CHAPTER 20

The next day we picked up the supplies needed to complete the mission from Mexico City. Transmitters and other technical equipment were easily purchased at a local Radio Shack inside the Plaza Lerota. After making a brief stop to visit with Bette's friend we decided to order take out from the fabulous Chilpoltes near the inn.

"McHenry's political buddies should start strolling in about 5 p.m. This gives them plenty of time to discuss business before pleasure. The female callers are scheduled to arrive no later than 6 p.m." Bette's eyebrows skirted up and down.

"You will enter the grounds when the gates open at 6 p.m. or you can try your athletic abilities by scaling the six foot wall. Which do you prefer?" she asked sarcastically.

"You leave me with little choice, if one doesn't work the other will have to and my levels of endurance will be slightly challenged," I scoffed. By now, the hour was drawing near and it was almost time to leave. I had been meticulously wired and things seemed to be moving along as planned.

We drove in silence while the sun submerged slowly into the horizon. With the evening hour came the rush of cool night desert air. Bette parked the car about a half mile down the dirt road inside a small wooded area. It would seem I would have to hike on foot the remainder of the way keeping my whereabouts concealed as best as possible. Bette would stay behind to decommission the cameras and security alarm, if needed. I fastened my headset then adjusted my weapon. I would have no problem blending into the fading light.

"Good luck, Alix." Bette said as she leaned over and planted a wet sloppy kiss on my cheek. Her eyes glistened with tears.

"Hasta luego," I replied then squeezed her hand.

"Why Alix, you've been working on your Spanish, eh?" she commented.

"Maybe…" I opened the door and started on my way towards McHenry's villa. This wasn't going to be easy and Bette had already agreed that if something should go wrong she was to leave Mexico immediately without me. I would not have her endanger her own life to save mine. Reluctantly, she made me a promise I hoped she would keep.

It didn't take long before I reached the mammoth set of gates located near the front entrance. I checked my watch and had a few minutes to spare. It was a beautiful sunset and my thoughts suddenly rushed to Sierra. How I longed to hold her in my arms and caress her beautiful face. Instinctively, my emotions crept in and unfortunately took over. I fought them desperately knowing this wasn't the best time for me to be reliving wonderful moments with Sierra. It wasn't until I heard the grinding sounds from the immense iron bars that I quickly snapped back to reality.

"Alix? Are you in?" I heard Bette whisper through my ear piece. Within that fraction of a second, I had almost lost my window of opportunity. Instinctively, I skirted behind the long black limousine which had just pulled up and coasted inside. The luxurious vehicle picked up speed as it hit the paved driveway. Frantically, I rolled onto the freshly cut grass to conceal my position.

It wasn't long before its doors flew open wide and exited the array of seductively dressed young women. There, standing in the flesh, to greet his bedding visitors, was the one and only, Judge Patrick McHenry. I knew I had to act fast in order to access the house without being detected. McHenry stood kissing and pawing as he personally escorted each one of them inside the hacienda. Muffled giggles could be heard while his hands lingered in subtle areas about their shapely bodies. Thinking quickly, I silently crept around the side of the villa to find safe haven through an unlocked window.

"Bette, the windows are locked!" I whispered frantically.

"Not anymore," she calmly replied. Once again, I cautiously pulled on the brass handle. This time, it gave way. Quietly, I slipped inside unnoticed. I eagerly closed the window after me and pulled out my pin point flashlight.

"I'm in," I whispered back. I quickly scanned the room to discover I was inside his library. Law book after law book stacked the repeating shelves.

"How ironic," I thought to myself. Laughter and muffled voices could be heard close by. It didn't take long before the party had begun. With caution, I gingerly eased the wooden door open just a crack. The magnificent foyer was huge. Two businessmen were already busily making sexual moves on their escorts. Their groping hands and slippery tongues crawled all over the bodies of both women who seemed to be enjoying the undivided attention. Unfortunately, neither one of the men was McHenry. Over to the side, a spiraling staircase swirled upward to a second floor.

"Gentlemen, please, please I have plenty of rooms for your convenience and your enjoyment!" announced McHenry from up above. Both men instantly looked up then nodded. Each couple held hands as they made their way up the winding set of steps.

"Bette, are you there?" I whispered into my headset.

"Where else would I be?" she returned sarcastically.

"I have to find McHenry and fast," I stated in desperation.

"Give me a minute," she replied sounding a bit frustrated. It seemed like a long time before Bette finally got back to me with the information I so desperately needed.

"I found him. He's in the master suite on the south side of the villa. It's the farthest room down the hall. You'll have to pass a couple of other rooms so be on guard, Alix," cautioned Bette.

"Great," I mumbled to myself. As I lingered hesitantly out into the foyer, I instinctively dimmed the blazing glass chandelier. With any luck, all five men would be permanently distracted with the flaunting ladies of the night. I moved gingerly and stayed close to the paneled walls until finally I reached the top of the staircase. Upstairs, the corridor remained unusually dark. I used this to my advantage and hastily eased my way toward McHenry's room. As I neared the master bedroom, I could clearly hear the young woman's cries of ecstasy along with the ungodly grunts and moans emanating from vile mouth of Judge McHenry.

As the disgusting yelps continued on with sexual expectations, I gently turned the brass door knob to peer inside. Within the darken room, I could see clearly the naked Judge McHenry vigorously thrusting his manhood inside the local prostitute.

"Joder you duro!" she screamed.

"Sí! Sí!" he cried back. The repulsive vision before me actually made my stomach churn and my body shudder. As I quietly inched my way inside, I made sure I locked the door behind me. Suddenly, during mid-flight, McHenry decided to flip on his back with the young Mexican woman flailing on top. She screamed with delight and arched to meet his savage penetration.

"Hacer te sensación mi gallo dentro te?" he stuttered.

"Sí! Sí!" she bellowed with excitement. And just as they were about to simultaneously reach their ultimate climax; I decided to announce my unexpected arrival.

"Good evening!" I shouted loudly while aiming my 9mm Beretta directly at McHenry's head. With the rush of emotional arousal coupled with my obvious inappropriate timing, McHenry's unstoppable trip to the sky had just been canceled.

"What the hell are *you* doing here?" McHenry's narrow beady eyes filled with rage as he swiftly released himself from his intimate attachment to his lady friend. She, on the other hand, was terrified by my presence and pushed herself nervously against the mahogany headboard of the bed.

"Hacer no herida yo!" she cried with fear. Her hands went up to protect her face as she tightly curled her naked body.

"Shut up you whore!" McHenry's mighty hand came down and smacked her violently across the face. The impact sent the petrified woman off the side of the bed where she remained still and unconscious. As he turned to face me, I slowly released the safety latch on my gun.

"Don't even think about it, McHenry! I'm not one of your little playmates!" My hand was steady and he knew I would not hesitate to put a bullet right through his scull.

"Please, do us a both a favor, put on your robe," I commanded as I tossed him the garment. He reluctantly wrapped it around his sweaty body.

"Why, can't stand to see what you've been missing?" he taunted. I laughed and shook my head with repugnance.

"What do you want, Becker? I thought I got rid of you!" he hissed through gritted teeth.

"I want you to come back with me to the United States and stand trial; that's all," I replied honestly. He then burst out into a hysterical laughter.

"Are you crazy, woman? Why in heaven's name would I do such a thing?" McHenry's snickered attitude was beginning to rub me the wrong way.

"You're guilty and you know it, McHenry. I was sent to bring you back, so you can make this easy or hard." I took a slight step backwards. McHenry's devious grin said it all.

"If I decide to pick the latter..." But I didn't give him the chance to finish.

"You won't! Drink this or…" I tossed him the small green vial. Instantly, he snatched it from mid-air then shot it straight back at me. I immediately ducked as it sailed above hitting the wall shattering into a dozen pieces.

"Do you think I'm a fool?" he sneered.

"No, and I knew you wouldn't come easy, so I guess this means you made up your mind and decided to do things the hard way. I'll have to shot your sorry ass and drag it over the border." I adjusted the gun and aimed at his private area.

"Wait!" cried McHenry.

"Let's not be hasty," he panicked while waving his arms.

"What if I come peacefully?" he asked moving himself off the bed.

"You would do that for me?" I asked innocently knowing full well of his devious intentions.

"You may handcuff me and I will be your prisoner." McHenry held out both of his arms straight in front of him. I knew I couldn't trust him, but I cuffed him just the same.

"Here's a pair of pants, put them on along with shoes." I threw the dark blue jeans on the bed and kicked over a pair of sandals.

"No shirt?" he questioned. I quickly glanced about the bedroom and saw a plain white t-shirt lying on the chair.

"You don't need one." McHenry gave me a stern look.

"You know, Becker, I am very agile for my age," boasted McHenry as if he was trying to impress me.

"McHenry, don't waste your breath. In fact, you disgust me as a human being. How do you live with yourself knowing you sent innocent people to prison? You bend the judicial system to fit your needs all in the name of money and power." My anger was beginning to build.

"How do *you* live with yourself knowing you're an abomination of the female species and a sexual deviant who preys on the same sex?" McHenry clumsily pulled on the sandals. For some odd reason, his words struck me hard. There were many times as I was growing up and throughout my law enforcement career that my lesbianism had rudely been shoved back into my face and down my throat.

"You're just jealous because I know how to please a woman better than you!" I chuckled. But it was within that instant of McHenry's ultimate rage when he violently threw his muscular torso directly at me. For a brief moment I was stunned until we both hit the hard wall. Together we dropped heavily upon the antique writing table breaking it completely in half. My head transmitter had been ripped away and I tried desperately to hold on to my gun, but it was no use. As my wrist cracked the side of the table, I felt the hot rush of radiating pain shoot up my arm. While I vigorously wrestled with his cuffed hands, McHenry thought he got the best of me. It was during our rumble on the floor, the beaten prostitute had awakened and decided to aid in the apprehension of this notorious and abusive man.

"Yo odio te!" she yelled as she aimed my gun at McHenry's head. Instantly, McHenry released his grip around my throat.

"Amante," replied McHenry softly. He slowly eased himself to his knees. Fury filled the young woman's battered face and without any warning she roughly kicked him in the ribs.

"Give me the gun; I promise I won't hurt you," I coaxed. The frightened prostitute turned it towards me. I cautiously stood up and took a step back.

"Él Él es un cerdo!" I exclaimed. Her hand shook with fear as McHenry began to inch closer in order to make his move. Wisely, she tossed me the weapon as McHenry roughly tried to grab the legs of his lady of the night. With precision and skill, I aimed and fired a direct shot into his left calf before he had a chance to reach the trembling woman.

"Aaaagh!" he yelped while rolling on the carpeted floor. The young woman instantly dashed across the room and stood behind me.

"Now look what you made me do?" I exclaimed. McHenry grasped his wounded leg as blood poured freely from the small hole.

"I need a doctor or I'm going to bleed to death!" he whimpered. I found my headset and tried to contact Bette.

"Bette, are you there?" Come in, Bette." I waited impatiently until the static cleared.

"You don't have to shout! I can hear you just fine. So, I guess you and the gimp need a ride, eh?" I could hear her cackling on the other end.

"You were watching the whole time?" I asked while glancing up at the security camera.

"Of course, do you think I would miss the show? Anyhow, there was nothing else to watch," she commented.

"We'll talk about this later. I need you to pick us up at the front door and hurry." I gagged McHenry then proceeded to bind his legs together. With the help of my new found friend, we were able to drag McHenry's struggling body down the steps and through the foyer where Bette was waiting patiently outside the door. It took all three of us to stuff his oversized body into the back seat of the car. Surprisingly enough, the grateful prostitute gave me a quick hug.

"Muchas Gracias!" she whispered in my ear.

"No problema," I responded. With that she vanished back inside the illustrious villa.

"A new amigo?" asked Bette smiling.

"I guess you could say that," I replied. McHenry had turned out to be a typical wimp and had passed out from the loss of blood.

"You think we should take him to a hospital?" questioned Bette. The road was dark and unfamiliar to me. Bette seemed confident with her directional senses.

"No, he'll live. We need to grab our things from the inn. I'll call Maria and have her send a private jet. I don't think we'll be able to get McHenry back on a local flight." We giggled together like school girls.

Maria was eagerly awaiting our call and had already sent a small unmarked plane with two armed officers to restrain McHenry along with a physician just in case. On the flight back, it was good to relax and enjoy the remainder of our time conversing like Bette and I used to do, so long ago. Before we landed at the airport, we made a promise not to the let years separate us ever again.

The bumpy landing into Hopkins Airport stirred my stomach. The weather was dismal as heavy rain clouds let loose with a cool spring shower. An armed police wagon escorted Judge Patrick McHenry back to prison where he would safely stay until his trial. It wasn't long before the lot of us was cozily sitting comfortably inside Maria and Sherrie's warm family room.

"I want to thank you both, Alix and Bette, for a job well done!" announced Maria.

"What do you think will happen to him?" asked Bette. Sherrie poured me another cup of hot tea.

"The indictments against McHenry are mounting and of course fleeing the country will not help his case one bit. They won't have a difficult time convicting McHenry. Even if he should, by some remote chance, enter into a plea bargain, he'll still be spending many valuable years behind bars." Maria looked more than confident with her summation. Bette remained quiet for a moment.

"How about you, Alix, what now?" she asked quizzically. I did not reply immediately. I sat quiet and reflected on my thoughts of Sierra.

"Alix, I need a good woman to head my investigative team. How about it?" Maria persisted.

"Thank you, Maria, for the kind offer, but I think I'm going away for awhile." I purposely left out all the details and everyone knew not to ask.

EPILOGUE

The clear blue Caribbean water was cool and crisp as it washed up lightly on the warm golden sand. But I remained unaware of the calming sea as my mind whirled around with visions of Sierra and I eagerly drowned myself inside with the realms of solace and despair.

It seemed like only yesterday when Sierra had been alive and full of life. My world was perfect then, with the love I had felt and so eager to offer. Perfect in the sense that I had finally found a woman to love and cherish. And now, those dreams had been shattered and destroyed by the hands of a notorious woman, who in her own twisted way, left behind only misery and utter hopelessness. My heart ached with grief and my burning eyes overflowed with agonizing tears, at the sweet and loving memories of my dear Sierra.

It wasn't long before total exhaustion overwhelmed my inner spirit, so I decided to saunter back to the old shack which remained hidden from the hustle and bustle of tourists and native islanders. As I neared the deserted hut, I noticed a strange, but alluring light drifting from the front battered widow. It seemed to mysteriously call out to me as if to welcome a lost soul back home.

With immense curiosity, I cautiously crossed the sagging porch and gently pulled on the tarnished handle of the salt eaten door. My tired and swollen eyes frantically tried to adjust to the beckoning and eerie glow. Suddenly, my racing heart skipped a beat at the sight of the burning candles upon the worn and stained ceramic sink.

There, only a few short feet away, quietly sat a shadowy figure of a woman. I hesitated for just a brief moment, and as the warm night breeze fluttered through the open window, I instantly became overcome with a pure sense of peace. Slowly, the ominous shape rose from the wooden chair as if to greet me.

"Who…are you?" I whispered with a trembling voice.

"I am who you've been waiting for," replied the mysterious woman in a soft spoken tone. Instantly, I recognized the voice and knew deep inside my ears must be deceiving me.

"The woman I have been waiting for is…dead." I immediately closed my eyes and knew this couldn't be real. Once again, her soothing voice floated back again as light as a sigh.

"She is not dead. She has been with you the whole time, in your mind and within your heart, where you have kept her safe from harm." My eyes flew open wide to gaze upon the mesmerizing essence as it drew near.

"Sierra! You're alive!" I cried out with joy. Then suddenly through the angelic streams of bursting moonlight that radiated from the redeeming heavens above, Sierra tenderly touched my tear stained cheeks and gently eased my tormented soul.

Love can often be taken for granted. It is the means by which we exist with one another in this man-made chaotic world. It is a reflection of the heart and the soul. Fate, in its pretentious and distorted way, had granted me a second chance, not only at love, but also at life itself. This time, I intended to hold on and never let go.